THE INVISIBLE MAN

P.F. FORD

To my amazing wife, Mary – sometimes we need someone else to believe in us before we really believe in ourselves. None of this would have happened without her unfailing belief and support.

1

Saturday 14th February 2017

THERE WAS a terrifying screech of metal on tarmac as the overturned car skidded along the road, sparks flying out behind it. Then, as the car finally came to a stop, the screeching was replaced by the rhythmic thrumming of a wheel spinning uselessly, until finally there was just eerie silence, punctuated only by the metallic ticking as the hot engine and exhaust pipe began to cool.

To his great surprise, he seemed to be unhurt, but the car was upside down, which meant he was hanging upside down from the driver's seat, held by his seat belt. His head had been protected from the road surface by the roll-over bars which had recently been fitted for precisely this scenario. A 1960s open-topped sports car was a beautiful thing to drive, but safety had never been a significant feature back in those days.

He became aware of a faint splashing sound, and the sudden whiff of petrol was enough to rouse him into action. After a brief struggle he managed to release the seat belt, and with the extra strength his fear had generated, he lowered himself to the road.

In the darkness, he could barely make out his passenger, but she had not been wearing a seat belt, so he was in no doubt she must be dead. It had never been his intention for anything like this to happen, and he suffered a moment of panic wondering how he was going to explain it, but then he had an idea. Sad as it may seem for someone so young to lose their life, this outcome might prove to be for the best. With any luck, he could manipulate the situation to hide his involvement.

He crawled out through the gaping hole where the door had been, his gloved hands protecting him from the debris of the shattered windscreen, then turned and crawled back inside, just far enough to enable him to reach the girl. For one final time, and in entirely different circumstances to usual, he appreciated her diminutive size, which helped him to quickly manoeuvre her small body across from the passenger side, as he backed out again.

He decided he didn't need to be too fussy; with petrol leaking, it was likely the car would catch fire and when that happened there wouldn't be much left of her, or the car. A few seconds later she was positioned on the driver's side, and he took a moment to sit back and admire his handiwork and ingenuity. As he did so, there was a familiar "ping" as her mobile phone gave notification of a message received. After a hasty search of her coat pockets, he found the phone and then scuttled away from the car.

Fifty yards away under the solitary street light that lit up this part of the road, he stopped to check the phone. He removed the battery and threw it as far as he could towards the distant trees, then put the rest of the phone back together, turned around, and threw it as far as he could in the other direction.

Then he started to run towards the woods on the other side of the road...

2

Dave Slater leaned back, balanced on the back legs of his chair, took careful aim at the wastepaper basket and launched the sheet of paper he had just scrunched into a ball. The missile bounced on the edge of the basket and joined the twenty-two others scattered across the floor.

'This is ridiculous,' he said.

Norman tore his eyes away from the small TV they were watching and stared at the rubbish all over the floor.

'I don't understand how you can be so good at darts, and yet be complete crap at getting a ball of paper into a bin.'

'It's my superpower,' said Slater. He took his feet from the desk and dropped his chair back onto all four legs.

'We could always play darts,' suggested Norman.

'No offence, Norm, but beating you over, and over, is every bit as boring as watching those crappy daytime TV repeats.'

Norman turned back to his TV show.

'Look,' said Slater, 'I know you don't want to talk about it, Norm, but we can't put it off any longer.'

Norman sighed and aimed the remote control at the TV, clicked the button, and watched as the picture shrank into the centre and then disappeared. He tossed the remote onto his desk and turned to face Slater.

'I know you're right,' he said, gloomily. 'I just keep hoping someone's going to walk in that door with an outstanding job, and that'll be the one that gets the ball rolling, you know?'

'I know, mate,' said Slater, 'and I'm sorry it hasn't worked out the way we wanted, but we have to face facts and be realistic.'

'How long has it been now?'

'Two weeks and three days since our last job. I don't know about you, but if we're going to sit around doing nothing I'd rather do it at home and not have to pay for this place.'

Norman sighed again.

'I was sure those adverts, on the back of that story in the newspaper, would bring some work in,' he said.

'Yeah, well, we'll have to put that down to experience,' said Slater. 'I think, if we're honest, it was always going to be a risk trying to find enough work in a small town like this.'

Norman cast an eye around the office.

'What are we going to do with all this stuff?'

'I dunno,' said Slater. 'I don't want any of it except my laptop. Maybe we can sell it. Anyway, we can decide that later.' He stood up. 'Come on, get your backside off that chair. Let's go down the pub and celebrate.'

'Celebrate what?'

'Finally opening our eyes to the truth, and admitting defeat.'

Norman got slowly to his feet. He appreciated Slater was trying to cheer him up, but he didn't feel they had anything to celebrate.

'Should we be celebrating defeat?' he asked.

'Maybe you're right,' said Slater, heading for the door. 'So let's celebrate something more positive, like making a decision. Of course, you can always stay here and be miserable if you prefer.'

Norman was finding it difficult to find anything to be cheerful about, but there again, he wasn't going to refuse a free lunch. He jumped to his feet and scuttled after Slater.

. . .

SLATER JUMPED INTO HIS CAR, started the engine and pressed the button to lower his window.

'Let's get some fresh air circulating through here,' he said. 'Maybe it will wake us up.'

As he drove slowly towards the car park exit, a car turned off the road and into the car park. He pulled over to the left and stopped to allow the car into the car park, but instead of driving past it stopped alongside him, the driver's window slid downwards, and a worried-looking woman stared uncertainly at him.

Slater smiled.

'Can I help you? You look a little lost.'

'I'm not sure I'm in the right place,' she said. 'I'm supposed to be looking for some detectives.'

Slater couldn't hide the surprise on his face.

'Really?'

'Yes,' she said, mistaking his reason for surprise. Then, taking a quick look at her surrounding, 'But this isn't exactly the sort of place you'd find a detective is it?'

'Actually, it is,' said Slater, grinning widely, 'and you've found them.'

'I have?'

'Slater and Norman at your service.'

'Really? Thank goodness,' she said, flustered. 'I need your help.'

'It'll be a lot easier to talk in our office,' said Slater. 'Follow me.'

He slipped his car into reverse and carefully made his way back to the space he had vacated just two minutes before.

'How weird is that?' said Norman. 'Another minute and we would have missed her.'

'Yeah, it was lucky, wasn't it?'

'Maybe it's fate. Perhaps she's the one we've been waiting for.'

Slater rolled his eyes.

'Yeah, right,' he said, slipping from the car.

The woman followed and parked next to them.

Slater left Norman to escort her into the office while he went on ahead and unlocked the doors.

3

Norman fussed around the woman as she climbed from her car.

'My name's Norman Norman.' He offered a hand, and she shook it.

'Lizzie Becker,' she said.

She was a small woman, and what Norman would describe as a neat and tidy dresser. He guessed she was around forty, but the lines on her face suggested the last few years hadn't been her happiest.

Norman indicated their office.

'Won't you come this way, Mrs Becker.'

'Call me Lizzie,' she said, hesitantly, then looked around startled as Slater noisily opened the office door.

'That's my partner, Dave Slater,' explained Norman.

Slater shook her hand as she entered the office, and indicated the small informal seating area.

'Please, come and sit down,' he said.

She looked uncertain, as though she was having second thoughts.

'Perhaps I shouldn't have come. I have thought about it before, but I never quite had the courage.'

'Lizzie, I'm sure you wouldn't have come to find us for no reason,' Norman assured her. 'Besides, you're here now...'

Norman's words seemed to be enough to strengthen her resolve. Nodding her agreement, she made her way across the room and took a seat. She swallowed nervously as they joined her and Slater produced a notebook and pen.

'You see I've had this weird text message,' she began, then seemed to have second thoughts.

'I'm afraid we need a little more than that,' encouraged Norman, after a few seconds of silence.

'You're going to think I'm crazy,' she said.

Norman smiled, reassuringly.

'I very much doubt that,' he said. 'Anyway, we're not here to judge. We need you to tell us what your problem is, and we'll tell you whether we can help or not.' He indicated his partner. 'Dave's going to take some notes, but if we decide not to take your case for any reason, we'll be sure to destroy those notes. Is that okay?'

She nodded, her eyes wandering to Slater's notebook, then his face, and then back to Norman.

'Okay, Lizzie, you said you had received a weird text message.'

'That's right.'

'Can you tell us what was weird about it?'

'It was from my daughter,' she said as if that explained everything.

'And that's weird, because...?'

'It's weird because she died two years ago.'

Norman's mouth formed a silent, surprised, "O", and Slater's pen stopped mid-word.

'Can you say that again?' asked Norman, tentatively.

She seemed to be staring at Norman but seeing through him, as if into some personal nightmare. Her shoulders raised as she heaved an enormous sigh, and when she spoke, her voice was almost a whisper.

'Just over two years ago our daughter went out for the afternoon. She told me she was going over to her boyfriend's house. His name is Mickey Crothers. He wasn't a boyfriend, in the real sense, she just called him that. The Crothers were old family friends. Mickey's mother and I were in hospital together when the children were born, and they grew up together. They lived in the same village as us, Lower Winton. Mickey was often at our house, or Lilly was over there. We were at opposite ends of the village, but it's only a five-minute walk through the woods.'

'On that day she told me she was going to Mickey's, so I wasn't worried about her, but then come the evening I started to get a bit concerned. I thought maybe she would be staying for dinner, so I rang them to make sure, but there was no answer. I tried calling and texting Lilly, but her mobile phone must have been switched off.

'I tried not to worry, you know? I thought maybe they had all gone to the cinema or something. I was a bit annoyed, to tell the truth, because normally they would phone and let me know if they were going out somewhere, but they didn't, and by eleven I was getting distraught, so my husband took me over to their house.'

She stopped speaking and stared down at her hands. A big, fat tear rolled slowly down her cheek. Norman reached for a box of tissues, grabbed a handful and passed them to her.

'Take your time Lizzie,' he said, gently. 'We're in no hurry.'

She took the tissues and wiped her eyes. Then she gripped them tightly in her fists as she composed herself.

'When we got to their house there was no sign of anyone. I was beside myself by then, but we didn't know what to do for the best. Eventually, even though we thought we would probably be wasting their time, we called the police and reported her missing.

'It was well after midnight before someone came to our house, but by then they had found her. She had been in a car crash just five miles from home.'

'Oh, I see,' said Norman.

Another solitary tear slid slowly down her cheek.

'She died in the crash,' she said.

'Oh, my,' said Norman. 'We're sorry to hear that.'

There was an awkward silence. Norman looked at Slater, who shook his head.

'They said she had stolen the car,' continued Lizzie, suddenly. 'But

I couldn't believe that. She didn't have the first idea of how to drive, and she had never shown any interest in learning. Why would she at fourteen years of age? And she was a good girl. She would never have stolen a car, especially from Jason Crothers. He was a family friend, and she knew that the sports car was his pride and joy!'

Now she focused on Norman's face, a look of pure anguish on her face.

'The car had turned over,' she said. 'The roof was down, and she wasn't wearing a seat belt. They said she died instantly!'

She buried her face in her hands and sobbed loudly.

Slater's pen hovered over the page. He hadn't written a single word of what she had just told them, such was the intensity of her story. He exchanged a pained expression with Norman, who had apparently found watching Lizzie Becker relive her agony an equally uncomfortable experience.

'I'm sorry to hear that, Lizzie,' said Norman, passing her more tissues. 'If you want to take a break—'

She shook her head. 'No. I'll be all right in a minute.'

'That's okay,' said Norman, gently. 'You take as long as you need.'

'I'll make us all some tea,' said Slater, and made his way to the small kitchen.

An uncomfortable five minutes later she seemed to have regained her composure.

'I'm sorry,' she said.

'Don't be silly,' said Norman. 'Are you sure you're okay to carry on?'

'Yes. I'm fine.'

'This text message that's got you so upset,' said Norman. 'Can we see it?'

She fished her mobile phone from her bag, found the message and handed the phone to Norman, who studied it, and then passed it on to Slater.

Hi Mm, wn't be hme 2nt but dn't wrry styng with M xx

. . .

'DOES this message mean anything to you?' asked Slater.

Lizzie shook her head.

'Is this the sort of message Lilly would have sent?' asked Norman.

'Well, yes, but it can't have come from her, can it?' she said. 'It's not possible.'

'I'm not suggesting Lilly sent it,' said Norman. 'But I think we have to assume someone is trying to upset you. If that's the case then the more it seems like Lilly could have written it, the more it will upset you.'

'I see what you mean. Lilly wouldn't normally tell me she wasn't coming home, but it's definitely her style to omit all the vowels, and she always ended her messages with two kisses.'

'Did you say Lilly was fourteen?' asked Slater.

'Yes. That's what I mean when I say she wouldn't normally be telling me she wasn't coming home. She wasn't old enough to stay out without permission from me or her dad.'

Slater was still studying the message.

'This message was sent a week ago,' said Slater.

She looked surprised, but Slater couldn't be sure if she were surprised by the date, or by the fact he had noticed it.

'Er, yes, that's right. I tried to ignore it at first, but it's been playing on my mind so much I can't sleep. I had to do something about it.'

'Do you recognise the number this was sent from?' he asked.

'No. I tried calling it to see if I could speak to whoever sent it, but all I got was a message saying the number was unobtainable.'

'What do you think this is, Lizzie?' asked Norman.

'I think it's some evil person playing a nasty trick.'

'Can you think of anyone who might want to do that to you?'

She frowned and shook her head. 'God, I hope no-one I know would stoop so low.'

'Have you been to the police about this?' asked Norman.

She shook her head again.

'I'm sorry,' she said, 'but I lost faith in them when they persuaded the coroner to agree it was death by misadventure. Because of them, I had to bury my little girl with everyone thinking she was a car thief!'

The last sentence was almost shouted, such was her anger, and there was an intense silence when she finished speaking. Guiltily she looked at them both in turn.

'I'm sorry,' she said, sheepishly. 'It's just that-'

'I think we both understand,' said Norman, 'and you don't owe us any apologies.'

'I'll just take a photo of this text message,' said Slater, 'and then you can have your phone back.'

'Do you think you can find out who sent it?' she asked.

'I have a friend who does tech stuff for us now and then,' said Norman. 'He's a bit of a genius. If he can't find where this came from, no-one can.'

Norman was referring to his friend, and technical genius, Vinnie. Normally Slater would balk at the idea of using Vinnie, whom he considered a hacker, but on this occasion, he wasn't going to argue. As Norman had stated, if Vinnie couldn't do this, no-one could.

'What happens now?' asked Lizzie. 'Do I pay now? I can afford it, you know.'

'These are our terms,' said Norman, handing her an envelope. 'You make your way home, then read these, think about it, and get back to us if you want to proceed. In the meantime, we'll do a little preliminary work, then we'll be ready if you want us to investigate.'

'But I already made my mind up,' she said. 'I want you to do it.'

She slipped a photograph from her handbag and passed it to Norman. The photo showed Lizzie Becker and a pretty, dark-haired girl. They were hugging and laughing at something.

'This was taken a few weeks before she died. Does she look like a car thief?' she asked.

Norman passed the photograph to Slater.

'I can see this is an emotional issue for you, Lizzie,' he said. 'I think you need to go home and think—'

'I've had over two years since the accident, and a week since the text to think about it,' she said, adamantly. 'I don't need any more time. I want your help.'

'WHAT DO YOU THINK?' asked Norman, once he had escorted Lizzie Becker out to her car and she had driven off.

'I think someone must have a seriously twisted mind to have sent a text message like that to a bereaved mother,' said Slater. 'But I think it's weird she waited a week to do something about it.'

'Yeah, but she knew it couldn't be from her daughter, so I can see why she thought it must be some crank. Maybe she thought if she ignored it they would leave her alone, but then she found it was impossible to ignore.'

'Yeah, you're probably right about that,' agreed Slater. 'By the way, I think using Vinnie is a good call.'

Norman's eyebrows shot upwards.

'You do? Wow, that's a first,' he said.

'That doesn't mean I think we should use him all the time. I think it's a case of horses for courses, and in this instance, he's our best shot.'

Norman recognised this was a significant admission for Slater to make, so he decided he shouldn't antagonise the situation with any smart remarks.

'I'll give him a call and see if he can spare a couple of hours,' he said.

Slater headed for his own small office.

'While you're doing that, I'm going to see what I can find out about this car crash.'

4

It was almost an hour later when Norman joined Slater.

'Vinnie thinks the number must belong to a Pay As You Go sim card,' he said.

'Does he think he can track it down?'

'He says it's no problem as long as the phone is live. Of course, if it's switched off, its a different ball game. But you know Vinnie; give him a challenge, and he'll rise to it.'

He peered over Slater's shoulder at his monitor.

'How are you doing here?'

'According to the press reports, the car Lilly Becker is alleged to have stolen was a 1966 Austin Healey 3000 sports convertible, owned by sports car enthusiast, Jason Crothers who, as Lizzy said, was a family friend of the Beckers.'

'Even I'm not old enough to remember their heyday,' said Norman, 'but I seem to recall they were considered pretty hot back then.'

'Yeah, that's right, and enthusiasts still race them even now,' said Slater.

'How did Lilly manage to steal the car?'

'As Lizzie told us, the families were friends, and Lilly and Mickey were often at each other's houses.'

'So she would have known about the car,' suggested Norman.

'That's right. The story is Lilly was in the house on her own and decided to take the car for a spin. On the way back she lost control, and it turned over. A roll-over bar was fitted to the car, but as it was an open top, there was nothing else to protect her when she hit a tree, and the car turned over. She had no seat belt on, so she had no chance.'

'Poor kid,' said Norman.

Slater eased his chair back and stretched.

'If this case landed on your desk, what would be your first question?' asked Slater.

'How d'you mean?'

'Well, we just stood next to Lizzie Becker. How tall would you say she was?'

'She's not very big. I guess about five feet four.'

'Right,' agreed Slater. 'So, going by that photo Lizzie gave us, how tall was Lilly?'

'No more than five feet at best.'

'Exactly.'

'Jeez,' said Norman. 'I see what you're getting at.'

'This car was built in the sixties, right. It was pretty powerful and would have weighed over a ton. And power steering didn't exist.'

'You think a small fourteen-year-old girl wouldn't have the strength to keep hold of a steering wheel if it was suddenly wrenched from her hands. But that's probably why she crashed.'

'Sure,' said Slater, thoughtfully, 'but my question is, would she have had the strength to drive it at all?'

'I'm sure they would have considered that,' said Norman. 'What do the reports say?'

'All the reports I've found say the police found no evidence another person was involved, and Lilly was in the driving seat when she was found.'

'There you go, then,' said Norman. 'Obviously, she did have the strength to drive it.'

'Not necessarily,' insisted Slater, stubbornly. 'I'm no expert, but I think we should take a look at one of those cars. I mean, nowadays you can adjust the seats, steering wheel, and who knows what else, but I don't think that was possible back then. Would someone as small as Lilly even be able to reach the pedals? And don't forget, according to Lizzie, Lilly had no idea how to drive and had never shown any interest in driving.'

'I can see what you're saying, but if there was no-one else involved...' Norman left the rest unsaid. 'You said she was in the house on her own; how did that happen?'

'It seems the Crothers family was away when the accident happened, but Lilly had a key. She used to go in and feed their two cats whenever the family were away.'

'So she was trusted by the Crothers?'

'Yeah,' said Slater. 'Apparently, she'd been feeding the cats for a couple of years without a hint of trouble which makes me wonder why such a well-behaved kid would suddenly do something like that?'

'But it happens, doesn't it?' said Norman. 'No-one's perfect. Don't forget she lied to her mother that day. Didn't she say she was going to meet Mickey Crothers? But if she were feeding the cats, she would have known the family were away, right?'

Slater sighed.

'Yeah, that's true enough, but even so, there must be an explanation for her behaviour. It seems so out of character.'

'Maybe she had another boyfriend apart from Mickey, and he put her up to it,' suggested Norman.

'So, where is he?' asked Slater.

Norman pursed his lips. 'Perhaps he didn't have the guts to face up to what had happened, and he ran away.'

Slater said nothing.

'Well, I wouldn't get hung up about it,' said Norman, patting his shoulder. 'I don't like it any more than you do, but it looks as if there wasn't much doubt about what happened. Besides, we're only supposed to be trying to find out who sent a malicious text to Lizzie Becker.'

Slater rose from his chair.

'Yeah, I suppose you're right,' he agreed, 'but there's nothing we can do about that until Vinnie locates that phone for us.'

'So what do you want to do in the meantime?'

'I figure it wouldn't do any harm to learn a little more about Lilly, and Mickey Crothers might be able to help with that.'

'I suppose it wouldn't hurt to get a little background,' said Norman. 'I'll give them a call and see if they'll let us speak to Mickey.'

5

'Mrs Crothers? My name's Norman Norman, and this is my colleague Dave Slater. I'm sorry to arrive unannounced. I've been calling, but your phone doesn't seem to be working. It just rings and rings.'

'The phone doesn't work because I unplug it to stop nuisance calls,' she said, pointedly. 'What do you want?'

'We're private investigators looking into an incident involving Mrs Lizzie Becker.'

'What is that woman trying to blame us for now? I haven't set eyes on Lizzie Becker since her daughter stole my husband's sports car. Whatever has happened now has got nothing to do with me.'

'Actually, we were wondering if we could come in and have a word with your son.'

'My son? I might have known the Beckers would try to drag his name through the mud if they got half a chance.'

'As far as I'm aware, no-one has accused your son of anything,' said Slater. 'We wanted to ask him about Lilly Becker.'

'What for?'

'We just want someone who knew her to give us a little insight into what she was like.'

'What's to know? She went bad, stole a car, and got what was coming to her.'

Slater stared, open-mouthed.

'What?' she said. 'Don't expect any sympathy from me. We trusted that girl. We treated her like one of the family, and look at how she repaid us.'

'Does your son feel that way? We understand they were pretty close.'

'I don't know what he feels. He never talks about that girl or what happened to her.'

Slater and Norman exchanged a look.

'If you wouldn't mind,' began Slater, 'we'd just like to come inside and ask him a few quest—'

'Certainly not!' she snapped.

'Perhaps you could ask him what he thinks.'

'That will be difficult,' she said, with a triumphant smirk on her face. 'My son's not here. He's gone to be with his father for a few days.'

'Oh. Your husband's not here?' asked Slater.

'That's none of your business,' she snapped.

'Can I ask where he is?'

'No, you cannot!'

'Marriages end, people divorce,' said Slater. 'It's nothing to be ashamed of.'

'I'm not ashamed,' she snapped. 'I'm not the one who walked—'

'Ah, so he left. I'm sorry, and you're right, it is none of our business,' said Slater. 'I didn't mean to pry.'

'You said you were a private investigator,' she hissed. 'That's what you people do, isn't it?'

Slater couldn't deny there was an element of truth in what she said so he chose not to argue.

'He moved to somewhere out of the way. He doesn't live here any more,' she said, red-faced. 'There, I've said it. Is that enough for you?'

'That's okay,' said Norman, amiably, 'We don't mind travelling to speak to your son.'

'I forbid you—'

'Yes, but maybe his father won't be so difficult—'

Her nostrils flared, and her face began to redden.

'Difficult?' she shrieked, her eyes blazing. 'How dare you! I'm just looking after my son's best interests.'

Norman was going to explain that wasn't actually what he was going to say, but when he looked into her eyes, he could see it would be a waste of his time.

'Maybe if you could tell us where we can find your husband, we could ask him what he thinks. If he agrees with you, then fair enough, we'll have to think of something else,' suggested Slater.

'I can assure you he will agree with me.'

'Yes, but if you could tell us where to find him, we can make sure,' Slater insisted.

Suddenly she didn't look quite so sure of herself.

'You do have an address for your husband?' asked Slater.

She shifted from foot to foot.

'Actually, I don't think I can tell you where he is.'

'But you just told us your son is staying with him,' said Norman, doubtfully.

'I said nothing of the sort. I said Mickey had gone to be with his father.'

'Is there a difference?' asked Norman.

'Yes, there is.'

'You don't know where your husband is, do you, Mrs Crothers?' asked Slater.

A look of great distaste crossed her face, but she wouldn't look at either of them.

'It's a difficult situation,' she said, bitterly.

'So, you and your husband are what, divorced?' asked Norman.

'Separated.'

'Right, separated. But wouldn't you need to know where your husband is? I mean you have a son. What if—'

'My husband walked out, not long after that wretched girl stole the car. He didn't want anything to do with us, and I damned well don't want anything to do with him. I haven't spoken to him since he left, and I don't care where he lives.'

'Don't you care where your son is?' asked Norman, innocently.

'Of course I bloody well do, but it's not that simple. Mickey has chosen to visit his father, and he has assured me if I call the police, or try to stop him, he will never speak to me again. I can't let that happen.'

'So your son has gone off on his own, and you have no idea where he is?'

'But I do know where he is,' she said, savagely. 'He's with his bloody father. It's just that he won't tell me where that is.'

'You could call his bluff and report him missing,' suggested Norman.

She shook her head.

'Don't think I haven't thought about it. But Mickey's done his homework. If I call in the police, they'll tell me that as long as he's happy and healthy, they won't intervene. They don't even have to tell me where he is!'

'Mickey must be sixteen, is that right?' asked Slater.

'Yes.'

'Then he's right. As long as his father's looking after him, Mickey can go to see him as often as he wants, and you can't stop him.'

She gritted her teeth but said nothing.

'But you can speak to Mickey on his mobile phone, right?'

'Yes, of course, but if you think I'm going to give you his number—'

'That's not what I was going to ask,' said Slater. 'Do you have a number for his father?'

She thought about it for a moment, then turned away and disappeared into the house. A minute later she re-appeared with a couple of business cards.

'Here,' she said, handing it to Slater. 'This is his business card. It's all I have. I assume he still works there.'

Slater looked at the cards.

'He has someone screen his calls,' she added. 'I presume that's so he won't have to speak to me, but you might have more luck.'

'Okay, thank you, Mrs Crothers—' began Slater, but the door had already closed.

Slater looked at Norman who grinned and shrugged.

'Beats me,' he said. 'If it was my son, and I was separated from his father I would want to keep in touch with the guy. I wouldn't mind the boy seeing his father, but I'm damned sure I'd want to know where he is.'

'You and me both,' said Slater.

'C'mon,' said Norman. 'Let's get out of here. I feel about as welcome as typhoid.'

6

'Let's try this phone number,' said Slater when they got back to the office. 'Maybe Jason Crothers will be a bit more amenable than his wife.'

He picked up the office phone, punched in the number, and waited as it began to ring at the other end.

'Hello,' said a female voice. 'Thank you for calling Keeling Security.'

'Oh, hi, my name's—'

'I'm afraid there's no-one here to take your call right now, but if you'd like to leave a message someone will get back to you later.'

'Bollocks,' muttered Slater, as he put the phone back on its cradle. 'It's an answering machine.'

'Really?' said Norman. 'But it's mid-afternoon. Surely the office must be open now.' He sat at his desk and began tapping at the keyboard of his laptop.

'When she said he has the calls screened I thought she meant someone answered it for him, not that he was using a bloody machine,' said Slater. He tried the number again but, as before, he was confronted by the same answering machine.

Norman had found what he was looking for, and now he turned to Slater.

'Can I see that card?' he asked.

Slater passed him the card.

'That's funny. This number isn't listed on the website.'

'Maybe they don't list mobile numbers,' suggested Slater.

'Yeah, maybe, but even so, he's a company sales director. He would want to be contactable. If he wanted his calls screened wouldn't he use a secretary to do that? An answering machine might be okay at night, but using one during the day implies a one-man band.'

Slater sighed. Of course, Norman was right.

'I'll tell you another thing,' added Norman. 'This is quite a big security company. There's no way they wouldn't be open this afternoon.'

He picked up the phone and pressed the redial key. He listened as it rang, and waited until the voice began to speak. He cut the call and went through the routine again, then ended the call, and passed the handset to Slater.

'Try it again,' he suggested, 'but this time, concentrate on what happens after the ringing stops, and before the voice starts speaking.'

Slater looked sceptical but did as Norman had suggested. He did it twice more, then handed the phone back to Norman.

'Those clicks,' he said.

'You heard it, right?' said Norman. 'It's redirecting to another line, and I bet it's got nothing to do with this company.'

Slater frowned.

'Why would he do that? Is he on the fiddle?'

'Perhaps he's set up his own company on the side, and he's skimming customers from Keeling Security.'

'That's a bit risky, isn't it?' asked Slater.

'I'll say,' said Norman. 'But I guess it can be worth the risk if you have the bottle. Years ago I knew a guy who did the same sort of thing. It took him about eighteen months, but eventually, he had enough customers to earn a good living. He quit his job, and his employers had no idea what he'd done.'

'What shall we do?' asked Slater. 'Call them, or pay them a visit?'

'It might be more fun if we can see their faces when we tell them,' said Norman.

'A job for the morning, then,' said Slater, with a beaming smile.

'In the meantime, I'll get Vinnie to check out the number we're being redirected to,' said Norman. 'Maybe he can give us a location.'

Slater looked at his watch.

'Are you okay if I head off home?'

'That face tells me you have a date, right?'

'If you mean, "am I seeing Stella tonight," yes I am.'

'Go on, then, enjoy yourself. I'll see you in the morning.'

7

Slater first met Detective Inspector Stella Robbins on a previous case. The relationship had been strictly professional in the beginning, but it had become something more after Slater had called to ask a favour one day, and they had now been going "steady" for about three months.

Stella had been attacked while on surveillance and had briefly resumed full duties (which is when she first met Slater), but it soon became apparent she had been severely traumatised by the attack, and she had been on desk duties for the last four months.

A consequence of the attack was her inability to relax when she was on her own with a man, especially in a car. It had taken weeks for her even to begin to trust Slater, a situation he had found challenging to say the least, but there was something about her that had made him stick around. Slowly but surely she had come to trust him, and even though there was still a long way to go she was far more relaxed with him now.

At 7.30 on the dot, he collected her from her mother's house in Winchester.

'So, how has your day been?' he asked, as he pulled away and headed towards town.

She sighed.

'They're going to fire me.'

'What do you mean "fire you"?'

'The official version is that my PTSD prevents me from carrying out my duties.'

'That's not the same as being fired, is it?' said Slater. 'It was a nasty attack. Someone tried to strangle you! No-one would have been able to shrug it off as if nothing had happened.'

'But this is my career. What am I going to do now?'

'What exactly did they say?'

'I have to attend a meeting at 11 am on Friday where they are going to,' she used her hands to make punctuation marks in the air, '"discuss my options".'

'So they're not actually going to fire you, are they?'

'It feels like it.'

'Maybe if you tried to be a little more optimistic it would help.'

She harrumphed. 'That's easy for you to say, it's not your life that's being torn apart.'

Slater had guessed this day was going to come. It was a sad fact that Stella was too traumatised to go back on front line duties and, consequently, it was only a matter of time before a decision had to be made about her future. He just wished there was something he could do to soften the blow.

'You're an experienced officer. I'm sure they'll find a place for you if they can,' he suggested.

'What, behind a desk doing paperwork? I've already had more than enough of that!'

Slater couldn't think of anything to say that would ease the situation, so he chose to keep quiet, and they continued their journey in moody silence.

THE GLOOMY ATMOSPHERE continued until they were sitting at a table in their favourite restaurant.

'I'm sorry,' she said. 'I shouldn't take it out on you. It's just—'

'Hey, look,' he said. 'You don't need to apologise. I understand how much you love your job, and I know how hard it must be for you right now. If you need to have a moan that's fine by me.'

She offered a sad little smile.

'You're very patient.'

'Don't kid yourself,' he said. 'I don't suffer fools.'

Now she smiled a much happier smile.

'Did I detect a disguised compliment in that statement?'

He smiled back at her.

'I did, didn't I?' she said. 'Should I be flattered you don't regard me as a fool?'

He reached for her hand. She observed his movements but resisted the temptation to snatch the hand away, and instead let him cover it with his. Then she looked up into his face.

'You are definitely no fool,' he said, 'so you must realise I'm here to support you in whatever way I can.'

She nodded.

'Yes, but what I can't figure out is why you're willing to do that.'

'I guess I must be a masochist.'

She chuckled.

'Yes, I'm sure you must be,' she said.

'There again,' he said, 'perhaps it's not that complicated. Maybe it's because I like you.'

They stared into each other's eyes, but then a waitress arrived to take their order, and the moment was lost.

'Aren't you going to tell me what you're working on?' she asked, once the waitress had gone.

'It's a bit of a weird one, but it's no big deal.'

'Weird in what way?'

'I don't think you'd be interested.'

'Of course, I'm interested.'

'Yes, I suppose you are, but I don't want you taking risks for us as you did before.'

She sighed and pouted.

'Don't look at me like that,' said Slater. 'You know what I mean.'

'What if I promise not to interfere?'

Slater studied her face. 'I honestly don't think you can resist the temptation.'

'Yes, I can. Besides, I probably won't have access to any information after this meeting on Friday.'

Slater thought this was probably true enough, and if she had no access she couldn't take any risks, could she?

'I'll tell you if you promise you won't go copying any case files,' he said.

'Scout's honour,' she said, sternly.

Slater knew she only wanted to help but, he wondered, could he trust her not to interfere? He studied her face again, but she was giving nothing away.

'A mother has received a text message from her daughter,' he said, eventually.

Stella looked confused.

'What's weird about that? Mothers get text messages from their daughters all the time!'

'Yeah, that's true, but this daughter died two years ago.'

Her eyes widened.

'Really? Oh, wow. Now that is weird!'

'Isn't it just?'

'How did she die?'

'Apparently, she stole a car, lost control, and turned it over. It was an open-top sports car, and she wasn't wearing a seat belt. She had no chance.'

'She stole it? How old was she?'

'Fourteen.'

'Fourteen! Good grief. That's a terrible waste of a young life. I'm surprised she even knew how to drive. I wouldn't have had a clue where to start when I was fourteen.'

'It's funny you should say that,' he agreed. 'I was thinking the same thing myself, but that's not what we're looking at.'

'It isn't?'

'No,' said Slater. 'Some sick bastard has sent a text to the girl's mother that looks as if the dead daughter sent it. We've got to find out who it was.'

'Did she report it to the police?'

Slater shook his head.

'Uh, uh. I'm afraid mum has no time for the police. She feels they were far too quick to label her daughter a car thief. She believes they got it wrong.'

'What do you think?'

'I'm not sure,' he said. 'As you said, would a fourteen-year-old know how to drive?'

Stella pulled a face.

'I'm afraid most parents feel we got it wrong when their little darlings are found guilty of committing a crime.'

'Yeah, I know,' said Slater. 'I've been there, too, remember?'

'So what have you found out so far?'

'We're not talking about this any more,' said Slater.

'Why not?'

'Because I'm still not convinced I can trust you not to get involved.'

She pouted again.

'I might not have anything else to do after Friday.'

'You don't know that for sure,' he said. 'As I said, you're a valuable asset to them. They'll want to find a place for you. Anyway, we're not talking about it anymore. What do you want to do at the weekend?'

Despite several further attempts to get him to talk that evening, Slater would not utter another word about his case.

8

Keeling Security occupied a massive barn conversion on a farm, a short distance from the M3 motorway, about 30 minutes from Tinton.

'There must be more money in security than I thought,' said Norman, as Slater pulled into a vacant parking space.

He stopped the car and looked across at the building.

'Do they own it, or rent it?'

'Apparently, Malcolm Keeling owns the farm, so I guess he owns the barn,' said Norman.

'He's not short of a few quid, then.'

'He started with nothing. He made his fortune from his business. It seems he's a bit of an innovator. Where he leads, the rest of the industry follows.'

'Well, good for him,' said Slater. 'I applaud anyone who has the drive to do something like that, but I wonder what he's going to think of Jason Crothers pinching his customers from under his nose.'

'Let's go and find out,' said Norman.

. . .

A HUGE PLANT-FILLED atrium occupied the centre of the barn and housed the reception area. As they entered, Norman stopped to breathe in the fragrance.

'Wow! It's like standing in an exotic greenhouse,' he said. 'This must be quite some place to work.'

A neatly dressed receptionist smiled to herself as she overheard Norman. It wasn't unusual for visitors to express such sentiments, and she knew they were right. It was a great place to work.

'Good morning,' she said, with a warm smile, as they approached her desk. 'Welcome to Keeling Security.'

'Good morning,' chorused the detectives.

'My name's Cara. How can I help you this morning?'

'We'd like to speak with Jason Crothers,' said Slater.

The receptionist allowed her smile to slip briefly into a frown but quickly recovered.

'I'm sorry? Who?'

'Jason Crothers.'

'I'm afraid we have no-one working here by that name.'

'Are you sure?' said Slater, surprised. 'Only we were told he's your Sales Director.'

'Harry Sillitoe is our Sales Director, but he's not here today.'

'That's strange,' said Norman. 'Jason even gave us his card.' He pulled the card from his pocket and handed it to her.

She stared blankly at the card, clearly confused, but she was a professional and refused to become flustered.

'I have only been here for a month, so I suppose it's possible I haven't met him yet,' she said, handing the card back. 'Could you excuse me a moment while I make a call? Perhaps you'd like to sit over there.' She indicated a seating area next to a small water feature.

'Sure,' said Slater.

They wandered across to the water feature and sat down where they could see Cara speaking to someone on the phone.

'What d'you make of that?' asked Norman, quietly.

'Very professional,' said Slater. 'She clearly has no idea who he is, but she didn't let it faze her. And, if she's as new as she said...'

'Yeah, but she must have a list of names. Maybe he doesn't work here anymore.'

'I guess that's got to be a possibility. Perhaps Malcolm Keeling figured out what he was up to, and kicked him out.'

Cara was heading in their direction, so they stopped speculating.

'If you wouldn't mind waiting, Keira Silver, the Sales Director's secretary, will be along to speak to you in a couple of minutes.'

They both smiled.

'Can I get you tea or coffee?'

'That's very kind of you,' said Slater, 'but we're fine, thank you.'

She offered them a sweet smile and returned to her desk.

'I wonder if Keira Silver was Jason Crothers' secretary,' said Norman.

The sound of heels clicking across the golden flagstones of the atrium made them both turn their heads. A dark-haired woman dressed in a smart suit was heading their way.

'I think this must be her,' said Slater, quietly. 'I wonder if she's going to be honest, or full of shit.'

'Judging by the expression on her face, my money's on "full of shit",' muttered Norman.

As she neared them, she broke into a professional smile and extended a hand.

'Good morning,' she said. 'My name is Diana Williams. I'm the Personnel Director.'

The announcement was unexpected, but the boys hid their surprise. They shook hands, then she invited them to sit down.

'Now then, how can I help you?' she asked, taking a seat opposite them.

'We're looking for Jason Crothers,' said Slater.

The smile disappeared at the mention of his name, but unlike the professional receptionist, she was unable to switch it back on.

'He doesn't work here,' she said, distastefully.

'We understood he is your Sales Director.'

'He was our Sales Director,' she corrected him.

'Oh, really? When did he leave?'

'It must have been about eighteen months ago.'

This was another surprise that went unacknowledged by both detectives.

'Did he leave under a cloud, by any chance?' asked Norman.

She turned her gaze in his direction, her face set like granite.

'Why would you think that?'

Slater took a guess.

'His wife mentioned an affair.'

Her eyes narrowed.

'I'm afraid I'm not prepared to discuss his reasons for leaving.'

'Right, said Slater. 'So we've established Jason Crothers doesn't work here anymore, and he left under a cloud.'

'I didn't say that.'

Slater smiled.

'You didn't need to,' he said. 'Can you tell us where we can find him?'

'I have no idea, and even if I knew, why would I tell you? Don't you know there are rules about privacy?'

Slater could almost see the barrier being swiftly erected between them. He thought perhaps a little exaggeration might ease the situation.

'Yes Mrs Williams, we do know there are rules about privacy, but we also know Mr Crothers' son is missing, and his ex-wife is worried sick. We need to find out if Mr Crothers knows where he is.'

This information seemed to have the desired effect.

'Oh. I see.' Her attitude had softened. 'That poor woman. As if she hasn't had enough to put up with.'

'So, can you tell us where we can find him?'

'No, I'm afraid I can't. Mr Crothers didn't leave any forwarding address. If he's not with his wife, I have no idea where he is.'

'Would anyone else here know where he is? What about the secretary he was having an affair with?'

'I didn't say anything about an affair!'

'Look, there are no idiots here,' said Norman, 'so let's stop playing games. A mother is worried sick about her son, and we think his father knows where he is. You can help us find him.'

She looked at Norman uncertainly, but then made her decision.

'I'm sorry, the answer's no. I will not have you upsetting my staff. And I can assure you before you ask, there is no-one here who would want anything to do with Jason Crothers.'

'Wow! That must have been some cloud he left under,' said Norman.

'I've already told you I'm not going to discuss it.'

Slater pulled the business card from his pocket and held it out to her.

'Did you know about this?'

She took the card.

'Good God,' she said.

'You mean you didn't know about this?' asked Slater.

'What? Well, er, no, I mean... Can I borrow this for a minute?'

'Sure,' said Slater. 'Be my guest.'

She got up from her seat, still clutching the card.

'Would you mind waiting? I'll be five minutes.'

They listened as the heels click-clacked back across the atrium.

'She knew, didn't she?' asked Norman.

'I thought so,' agreed Slater. 'But she wasn't expecting us to know. I'm surprised the receptionist didn't tip her off.'

'Maybe there's no love lost there,' suggested Norman. 'I have to wonder about that card though. If we're wrong about that and he wasn't kicked out for fiddling, what the hell did he do?'

'Well, we now know there was an affair.'

'Yeah, that was a good guess, and it was good of her to slip up and admit that,' said Norman. 'An affair doesn't always get you fired though, does it?'

'Maybe this is one of those companies that has a moral code of conduct.'

'But an affair wouldn't alienate everyone, would it?'

'Maybe there was more to it than that,' said Slater. 'Perhaps he bullied his secretary into an affair. One thing's for sure, Diana Williams isn't going to tell us what it was.'

'D'you think his wife knows he doesn't work here anymore?'

Slater thought for a moment.

'She knew about the affair, so if he lost his job over that, she must know, mustn't she?'

'But she handed you the card with his number on. Why would she do that, if she knew he wasn't working here?'

'Maybe she wanted us to find out.'

'Why not just tell us?'

Before Slater could reply, they heard the heels tapping their way back across the atrium. They turned and watched Diana Williams approach.

'Are you in a hurry?' she asked.

'That depends,' said Slater. 'If you're suggesting we have to hang around—'

'Malcolm Keeling would like to speak to you.'

'Now?'

She nodded. Slater looked at Norman, who nodded, too.

'Yes, okay, that might be helpful,' said Slater.

'Come this way,' she said.

They rose quickly from their seats and followed her across the atrium and out through the glass doors, where she turned to face them. Initially, Slater thought she was going to tell them to go away and never come back, but she merely pointed to a large farmhouse across a field from where they stood.

'Go back down the drive,' she said. 'Take the first right-hand turn, and follow it. It will take you along the edge of this field and on to the farmhouse. Malcolm is expecting you.'

She turned on her heel and walked back into the building, not even giving them time to thank her.

'This had better be good,' said Norman, as they climbed into the car.

'It must be good if the big boss wants to speak to us.' said Slater. 'Maybe we just hit the jackpot without realising it.'

9

As they approached the farmhouse, Malcolm Keeling appeared at the front door. A tall, willowy man, with dark brown hair greying at the temples, he gave them a friendly wave as they neared the house, then indicated they should park right outside the front door. Once the introductions were made Keeling took them inside, led them to his study, and settled them in two chairs. Then he took his place behind an enormous oak desk.

Another one with a barrier thought Slater, but at least this one was visible.

'Diana tells me you've been asking about Jason Crothers.'

Slater thought he could detect the faint trace of a lilt in his voice that suggested the possibility of Irish ancestry.

'That's correct,' said Norman. 'We're trying to locate his son, Mickey. Jason's wife is worried sick about the boy. She believes he's with his father. She's asked us to find Mickey and make sure he's all right. So we'd like to know where Jason is.'

'Yes, so would I,' said Keeling.

He picked up a business card from his desk. It looked like the one Slater had handed to Diana Williams.

'Can I ask you where you got this card?' he asked.

'Mia Crothers. She said it's the only contact details she has for him,' said Norman. 'But now we hear Jason doesn't work for you anymore, so we're confused.'

'There's nothing about which to be confused. It's quite simple. Jason doesn't work here anymore. What's confusing about that?'

'What's confusing is he's been fired, yet he's still authorised to use your company's business cards. How does that work?'

'Of course, he isn't! Anyway, these aren't our cards.'

'It's your company name,' said Slater, 'and your colours. What are they? Forgeries?'

Keeling sighed and shook his head.

'I admit they're similar, but they're not ours.'

'But you knew he was using them, right?' asked Norman.

Keeling stared at Norman for a few seconds as though he was trying to decide what to say. Finally, he sighed and then spoke.

'Yes, I knew.'

'So why haven't you stopped him? He is poaching your customers, isn't he?'

'But that's the strange thing. Jason hasn't approached a single one of our customers, and as far as I can tell, he's no longer active in the security business.'

'Have you any idea what he's up to?' asked Slater.

Keeling shook his head.

'I would ask him, but I have no idea where to find him. I've tried calling that number, and leaving a message, numerous times, but he never calls back. I suppose I can't blame him. I did fire him.'

Slater thought he could smell a rat.

'I have to say I find it unlikely a man as successful as you would turn a blind eye to a former employee continuing to pose as part of the business.'

Keeling glared at Slater.

'What are you implying?'

'I'm not implying anything. I'm just trying to understand why you haven't tracked Crothers down and stopped him. You're in the security business. You must know someone who could find him, but you haven't. I wonder if perhaps he knows something you'd rather he didn't know.'

'I don't know what you mean,' said Keeling, innocently.

'Can you tell us why you fired Crothers?' asked Norman.

'I thought you knew that; he took advantage of his position, and had an affair.'

'With Keira Silver?'

Keeling tried to hold Norman's gaze, but there was just the faintest flicker of acknowledgement, and Norman didn't miss it.

'We don't discuss what happens inside our business,' said Keeling. 'We've told you too much already.'

'But people have affairs all the time, don't they?' said Norman. 'If they were consenting adults, and it didn't affect their work, what's the harm?'

'When I need advice about how to run my business, I'll let you know,' said Keeling. 'In the meantime, I'll continue to do things my way. It seems reasonably successful.'

Norman bobbed his head. There was no arguing with that fact.

'I'm confused,' said Slater. 'Diana Williams said you wanted to speak to us, yet you don't seem to want to tell us anything.'

'It's taken me years to build this business, and I don't want you two creating a scandal that could ruin everything.'

'We're not trying to create a scandal,' said Norman. 'We're just trying to find the son of a mother who's going frantic with worry.'

'That's very noble,' said Keeling, 'but I fail to see how opening old wounds is going to help.'

'I'm not interested in your old wounds,' said Norman. 'But, if that boy is with his father, and someone here can tell us something that might help us find him, it is going to help.'

'The problem is no-one here seems to want to help us,' added Slater. 'That seems to suggest you all have something to hide.'

Keeling glared at Slater, again.

'I think we're done here,' he said.

'You think so, do you?' asked Slater. 'Because my gut tells me we've hardly got started.'

'I think you should leave, and I suggest you stay away from my business, and my employees.'

'ARROGANT PRICK,' observed Slater, as he slowly drove away from Keeling's house.

'He was never going to tell us anything, was he?' said Norman. 'He just wanted to get us away from the offices.'

'Yeah. I wonder what he's trying to hide.'

'Maybe Keira Silver knows.'

'Yeah,' said Slater. 'He tried hard not to show anything when you mentioned her name, but it was right there, just under the surface, wasn't it?'

'I think we should try speaking to her, don't you?'

'It can't hurt, can it?'

Norman searched through his notebook until he found the telephone number for Keeling Security and tapped the number into his mobile phone.

'Good Morning,' he said into the phone, a few seconds later. 'I'd like to speak to Harry Sillitoe please.'

'I'm afraid Mr Sillitoe is out of the office today, but I can put you through to Mrs Silver, his secretary, perhaps she can help you.'

'Yes, I'm sure she'll be able to help me,' said Norman. He looked at Slater and winked.

'Hello,' said a voice in his ear. 'This is Keira Silver speaking. How can I help you?'

'Good morning Keira. I'm sorry to call you like this but I need to speak to you, and I couldn't think of a better way.'

'Who are you?' The voice had raised an octave. 'What do you want?'

'Now please don't be alarmed. My name's Norman Norman. I'm a private investigator working with my partner to try and find a missing teenage boy. He's the son of Jason Crothers, and we think he might be with his father, but we're having trouble finding him. I was hoping you might be able to help.'

'Are you one of the two men who called here earlier?'

'Yes, that's right. You knew we were there?'

'Cara told me you were there, but Diana Willams wouldn't let me speak to you. Malcolm Keeling has forbidden me to speak to anyone about what happened.'

'I don't want to get you into trouble, and we don't need to know what happened. We only want to know where Jason Crothers is.'

'I'm sorry, I can't say any more. I have to go.'

'Oh. Really? We were rather hoping—'

She ended the call, and Norman sighed as he lowered his phone.

'No good?' asked Slater.

'She hung up. I got the feeling she would have liked to have said a lot more, but get this; Malcolm Keeling has forbidden her to speak to anyone about what happened.'

'Makes you wonder what did happen,' said Slater.

'Yeah, doesn't it just?' agreed Norman.

They drove on for another ten minutes, each lost in their thoughts until Norman's mobile phone began to ring. He accepted the call and raised the phone to his ear.

'Yo, Vinnie! How are you, my friend?'

A protracted call ensued, of which Slater could only hear Norman's half, much to his irritation, but eventually, Norman ended the call and slipped the phone back into his pocket.

'You could have put it on speakerphone,' complained Slater.

'Yeah, you're right, I could have,' agreed Norman, cheerily.

Slater waited for more information, but Norman simply stared out of the window.

'Is it a secret?' asked Slater.

'What?'

'Vinnie just called. I assume it was about this case, and as I'm your partner, I'm quite interested in what he had to say.'

'Oh, that. Yeah. Vinnie says he traced the redirect number. He knows where it's located. He's just going to text the address to me. I was going to tell you when the text comes in.'

'Sometimes you can be as annoying as Vinnie is,' said Slater.

Norman laughed.

'Vinnie was right. He said it would wind you up!'

'Ha, bloody, ha,' muttered Slater.

Norman's phone pinged as Vinnie's text message arrived. He found the text, and read it. He didn't recognise the address, so he fired up the car's Satnav and tapped in the postcode.

'Now that's handy,' he said.

'What's handy?'

'The address for this redirect number. We're almost going past it on the way back.'

'So what are we waiting for?' asked Slater. 'Let's go pay someone a surprise visit.'

10

The house they were looking for was in the middle of an enormous housing estate on the edge of Basingstoke. Slater hated these vast estates.

'Where's the imagination?' he complained. 'Every house is the same. We'd never be able to find the right house without Satnav.'

'You're right,' agreed Norman, looking around. 'And it's not just the houses, every road looks the same, too.'

'Here we go,' said Slater, as they rounded a bend, and he recognised the road name. 'It must be along here somewhere.'

'You have reached your destination,' announced the Satnav.

'There, on the left,' said Norman, pointing to one of the nondescript houses. 'Number 29.'

An attractive woman answered the door. Her hair was dyed an unnatural bright ginger, a colour that Slater felt was too close to orange for comfort. The half-smile she wore as she opened the door was rapidly replaced by a frown when she saw the two men standing on her doorstep.

'If you're Jehovah's Witnesses, I've told you before; I'm not interested,' she said.

Norman adopted his most placatory smile.

'It's okay,' he said. 'We're not Jehovah's Witnesses. We're Private Investigators.'

Her eyes narrowed.

'Private investigators? Then I'm even less interested.'

She went to shut the door, but Norman reached forward to stop it.

'Look we're not here to make trouble,' he said.

'What do you want then?'

'Are you Mia Crothers?' he asked.

The boys had planned their approach to this interview on the journey, agreeing Norman would lead but allowing him to play it as he saw fit. However, his unexpected opening question took everyone by surprise, and both the woman and Slater stared at Norman, puzzled.

'I think you've got the wrong house,' she said. 'My name's Summer Duval.'

Now Slater turned his puzzled stare on the woman, surprised by her exotic name.

'Oh,' said Norman. 'We must have been given the wrong information. We're looking for a man called Jason Crothers, and we were told you might be able to help us.'

She frowned.

'Who?'

'Jason Crothers.'

She studied Norman for a moment.

'Sorry. I've never heard of anyone called Jason Crothers.'

'Are you sure?'

'Of course, I'm sure. Do I look like someone who has a house full of men I don't know?'

Norman bit back his retort as Slater stuck a hand in his pocket and produced the business card he had kept.

'Maybe this will ring a bell,' he said and offered it to the woman.

She took the card, glanced at it, and then at Slater.

'All right,' she said, handing the card back to him. 'So now I know how to spell the man's name, but I still don't know him.'

She moved to close the door again, but Norman spoke before she could close it.

'But, don't you provide a telephone answering service for him?'

Her eyes widened, and her mouth flapped once or twice before she spoke.

'I don't know what you mean,' she said, defiantly.

Slater smiled.

'Oh, I think you know what he means,' said Slater. 'But, I wonder, do the police know about your little sideline?'

'You see, the thing is,' explained Norman, 'we know just how many redirected calls you receive every day, and we know your service isn't listed as a business.'

'We also know just how lucrative it can be,' added Slater, 'especially if your clients are ladies of a certain kind, or a little, how shall we say, dodgy?'

'We were wondering what the guys who deal with vice might think about your little sideline,' said Norman.

'If you have just one or two clients they might turn a blind eye, but if it's a lot more than that, and they're mostly working ladies, they might not be quite so lenient.'

'I don't know what you mean,' she stammered.

'Now, we all know that's not true, don't we?' said Norman.

The woman looked frantically from Slater to Norman, then stepped forward so she could see up and down the road. Satisfied no-one was watching, or listening, she stepped back through the front door.

'You'd better come inside,' she said.

They followed her into the house, where she showed them into a small dining room. Slater reached for a chair, intending to pull it from under the table and sit down.

'Don't bother,' she snapped, her hands on her hips. 'You're not going to be here long enough to get comfortable.'

He smiled and nodded his head. If that was how she felt, he was okay with that. He wasn't here to argue.

'Right,' she said, defiantly. 'What the hell is this?'

'We told you,' said Norman, 'we're just trying to find this guy Jason Crothers, but no-one seems to know where to find him.'

'We're not interested in what you do,' added Slater. 'We just need to find this guy.'

'And we were hoping, as you take calls from him, you might know where to find him,' finished Norman.

'But I don't take calls for him. I know the names of all my clients, and he isn't one of them.'

'Look, Summer, we already know you work for him. We dialled his number, and it redirects to a number which can be traced back to this house. How do you think we knew to come here?'

Her confidence faded slightly in the face of this damning evidence.

'But I don't know that name,' she insisted.

'I assume you know all the numbers that redirect to you,' said Slater.

'Well, yeah, I've got a list.'

He handed her the card again.

'Is this one of the numbers on your list?'

'Christ. You don't expect me to remember them all, do you?'

'But you could check it against your list,' suggested Slater.

'Why do you want to know?'

'A sixteen-year-old boy is missing-'

'Well, why didn't you say that in the beginning?' she said, and the atmosphere in the room changed instantly. 'Hang on a minute while I get my laptop.'

She left the room, and they listened as her footsteps thumped up the stairs and then, a few seconds later, thumped back down again. She was opening the laptop as she re-joined them.

'They're on a spreadsheet, so it's an easy search.'

She placed the laptop on the table, copied the number from the card into her spreadsheet, and clicked "search".

'You're right,' she said. 'It is one of my numbers.' She compared the name on the card to her spreadsheet. 'But this isn't the same name.'

'Can you tell us what name you have listed against that number?'

'I don't know if I should.'

'The guy's wife gave us that card,' said Norman. 'If this guy is up to something fishy he probably isn't calling himself Jason Crothers, he'll be using an alias. Just remember, that poor boy's life could be at risk.'

'Think how you would feel if anything happened to him and you could have helped,' added Slater.

They watched as Summer wrestled with her conscience.

'If anyone was to find out I told you...'

'We already told you we're not interested in your business, and we know how to keep quiet. No-one is going to find out, I promise,' said Norman.

She thought about it for a few more seconds.

'Now I think about it, this one's a pain in the arse,' she said. 'He never collects his messages on time, and he doesn't always pay on time. Yeah, sod it, why should I protect him?'

Having persuaded herself it was the right thing to do, she turned to Norman.

'He calls himself Josh Ludlow. At least, that's the name he gave me, but I don't have an address for him. I don't have an address for anyone.'

'How do you get paid by these people?' asked Slater.

'Mostly by cash, through the post. Makes it hard to trace.'

'What about Josh Ludlow?'

'Same thing.'

She suddenly realised she was probably saying more than she should.

'Anyway,' she said. 'I think you've got what you came for, and I'd rather you weren't here when my husband comes home.'

'Yeah, you're right,' said Norman. 'We should go.'

'I hope we can agree you won't be coming back,' she said as she showed them out.

'That depends,' said Norman, turning on the step to face her.

'On what?' she asked, defiantly.

'On you not having just given us a load of bullshit.'

Her self-assurance suddenly seemed to fade, but she still managed to slam the door.

'I'M sure it's not relevant, but d'you think that's her real name?' asked Slater, as they drove away.

'What's wrong with being called Summer?'

'Didn't you think it was a bit too exotic with that French-sounding surname?'

'I hadn't given it much thought,' said Norman. 'Maybe she thinks it goes with the dodgy business, but we have her address so it would be easy enough to check her out if you think it's important.'

'Important? God no, I don't think it so. I'm just wondering how a woman like that got involved with a guy like Crothers?'

'Perhaps he used to leave messages for call girls through her. Who knows, she might have been a call girl herself, and that's how they met.'

'It's a bit seedy using her for an answering service, don't you think?'

'Oh, for sure,' agreed Norman. 'It makes you wonder what he's really up to.'

'Whatever it is, you can be sure it's not legal,' said Slater.

The conversation was interrupted by Slater's mobile phone.

'It's Stella,' he said.

'If you want to stop I can get out, and you can talk in private,' suggested Norman.

'Don't be a tit, Norm, you're my best mate. She's not calling to whisper sweet nothings to me. There won't be anything I wouldn't want you to hear.'

'That may be so, but I think you should warn her if she's on speakerphone.'

Slater pressed a button on his steering wheel.

'Hi Stella, I'm driving so you're on loudspeaker.'

'Does that mean you have company? Hi, Norm.'

'Hi Stella,' said Norman. 'I offered to get out of the car, but he won't pull up.'

She laughed.

'I don't think that will be necessary. I'm not planning on saying anything exciting to him.'

'Hey,' said Slater. '"Him" is sitting right here, and you're supposed to be speaking to "him" and not to his passenger.'

'Okay, grumpy, I'll get straight to the point then. I can't make it tomorrow night, so can you come over tonight?'

'Yeah, okay, but I'm running a bit late. I'll be an hour or so.'

'Okay, I won't keep you if you're driving. See you later. Bye.'

There was a click, and she was gone.

'She doesn't beat around the bush, does she?' said Norman. 'Straight to the point and end the call. I like that, it's pretty special.'

'Yeah, you're right, she is pretty special,' said Slater.

Norman looked sideways at his friend and smiled to himself. He could have sworn Slater was sitting a little taller since that phone call.

11

When Slater arrived next morning, he was carrying something wrapped in a bag under his arm. He went straight through to his own office and put the bag on his desk, but before he could get back out, Norman elbowed his way in with two cups of tea.

'So how was the date?' he asked.

'Oh, you know. We went for a meal, that's all.'

'So Stella didn't hand anything over then?'

'Sorry?'

Norman nodded towards Slater's desk. 'The bag you brought in with you. It looks just the right size to be holding paperwork.'

'Ah. Yeah,' said Slater, guiltily. 'About that—'

'Has she stolen another file?' asked Norman. 'Jeez, she's gonna get caught one of these days, and when she does, she'll get fired. D'you want that on your conscience?'

'I didn't ask her to steal the bloody file,' said Slater. 'I told her I didn't want her getting involved at all, but she won't listen!'

'Well, then I suggest you stop telling her what we're working on.'

'That's what I am doing.'

Norman looked pointedly at the bag on Slater's desk.

'Then you're not doing it very well, are you?'

'She has a way of wheedling information out of me.'

'That'll be on account of her being a woman,' said Norman.

'No, it's not like that,' argued Slater. 'It's because she's a good detective. She knows how to ask questions.'

Norman grinned. 'Yeah, right. She knows how to play you is what it is.'

Slater's face had turned a healthy shade of red.

'Hey, don't be embarrassed,' said Norman. 'I get it. But even so, you have to stop her doing it.'

'Yeah, I know, but we've got the file now. What do you want me to do, burn it?'

'Hell, no. Now we've got it we might as well make use of it.'

'I had a quick look through it when I got home last night. It's not the whole file, just a map and a few bits she thought might help.'

Norman's phone was ringing.

'I'd better get that,' he said and headed for his desk.

Slater sat down and opened the bag on his desk.

'THAT WAS VINNIE,' said Norman a few minutes later. 'Whoever has the mobile phone that sent the text to Lizzie Becker switched it on for a few minutes this morning.'

'Does he know where it is?'

'He says it's only a few miles from here. He's emailing a map, but he says it will only show the area between the masts where the phone was at 10 am.'

'If that phone has moved we've had it, right?' asked Slater.

'Yeah, he's gonna try to keep tracking it and updating us.'

The sound of a notification ping from Norman's laptop told them the email had arrived.

'There we go. I'll print it out,' said Norman.

He went back to his laptop, opened the email, and clicked "print".

The printer began whirring away as Norman came back into Slater's office.

'It's in East Winton,' he said. 'Isn't that where Lizzie Becker lives?'

'Not quite, but it's not far from there,' said Slater, flipping back through the file he was reading. 'Yes. Here we are. The Beckers live in Lower Winton, but it's only a couple of miles from East Winton which is where Lilly had her accident.'

'That's a bit of a coincidence, isn't it?' said Norman, walking across to the printer.

He waited as the printer finished, took the printed sheet of paper and studied it.

'This is interesting,' he said, handing it on to Slater.

Slater stared at the map.

'Just outside the village. No houses.'

'Just trees, and grass, by the look of it,' said Norman. 'Maybe whoever it is was walking their dog or something.'

'They were lucky to get a signal out there,' said Slater.

As he stared at the map, Slater realised it was similar to the one in the file he was reading. He quickly flipped back through the file until he found what he was looking for, then held the map up against it.

'Here, look,' he said. 'This is right where Lilly crashed!'

Norman came around so he could lean over Slater's shoulder. He studied the two maps. On the map in the file, the crash site was marked on a sharp bend a couple of hundred yards outside the village. The triangle indicating the location of the mobile phone on Vinnie's map had the same curve right in its centre.

'Now that is a coincidence,' said Norman.

'Lilly's mobile phone was never found,' said Slater, looking around at him.

Norman looked at him, doubtfully.

'What? Are you suggesting this is her phone?'

'It can't be; the numbers are different. I think it's a bit of a coincidence, though, don't you?'

'Did she even have her phone with her?'

'It wasn't found at the scene, but then it wasn't found at home either. Her friends and family agree she took it everywhere with her, so there's no reason to think she didn't have it with her that day.'

'Let's not complicate things,' said Norman. 'The numbers are different, right? So, it can't be her phone.'

'Okay, okay,' said Slater. 'I was just making an observation.'

'Right. Observation noted,' said Norman, 'but I think it should also be dismissed.'

'Fair enough,' said Slater. 'What do you want to do about this mobile now it's live? Do you want to head out there?'

'I suppose it wouldn't hurt to take a look, although if it is a dog walker, they could be long gone by the time we get there.'

'It wouldn't hurt to see the crash site, would it?' said Slater. 'And it's not as if we've got much else to do.'

'Yeah, I suppose so, and I guess Vinnie will update us if that phone moves.'

Slater closed his folder and grabbed the map.

'Right then, let's go.'

12

Slater had been quieter than usual since their earlier discussion about Lilly's mobile phone. He hadn't said a thing during the ten minutes since they had driven away from the office, and now Norman was beginning to feel uncomfortable. It was time to speak up.

'Okay,' he said finally, 'I don't know what's up with you this morning, but your mood has been going downhill ever since I didn't agree with your new theory. If you have a problem with that, spit it out so we can deal with it.'

'I don't have a problem with that, and it's not a big deal you don't agree with me. We often disagree about these things. It's how we work.'

Norman pursed his lips, thoughtfully.

'Do you have a problem with Stella? If you have, tell me to mind my own business, and I'll sit it out. At least I would know what's up.'

'I don't have a problem with Stella.'

'In that case, it must be me,' said Norman.

Slater said nothing but stared resolutely ahead.

'Okay,' said Norman. 'That silence tells me everything I need to know, but you need to understand I'm not prepared to spend all day with you if you're going to sulk, and I'm not going to play some stupid guessing game to find out what's wrong. So, how about you tell me what I've done, and then we can talk about it, and if I'm in the wrong I'll apologise.' He turned to look at Slater. 'Does that sound fair?'

Slater sighed. 'It's not you,' he said, at last, 'at least not exactly.'

'What's that supposed to mean?'

'It's Vinnie.'

Norman's eyebrows shot up.

'Vinnie? Jeez, you're not off on that hacker thing again. I thought you were okay with using him now.'

'No, it's not the hacker thing, and I am okay with using him. Well, no, that's not true. I was okay with using him.'

'But he's been seriously helpful.'

'Yeah, I know, Norm, but that's the problem. He's too bloody helpful.'

Slater would have preferred to have been facing Norman, but as he was driving, the best he could do was an occasional glance in Norman's direction.

'I'm not sure I understand what you mean,' said Norman.

'Look at the last case we had. It was Vinnie who discovered the false IDs, and it was Vinnie who tracked the mobile phones. Without Vinnie, we would still be working that case and getting nowhere.'

'Yeah, but isn't that a good thing?'

'And now look at this case,' continued Slater. 'Once again, we're relying on Vinnie. We're supposed to be the bloody detectives, and we're relying on your pet hacker to solve all our cases!'

Norman rolled his eyes.

'Oh, here we go,' he said. 'You see, it is the hacker thing again. I keep telling you he's never done anything criminal, but you don't seem to want to listen.'

'Norm, you're missing my point. I promise you it's not the hacker thing, and I believe you when you say he's not a criminal. I'm okay with that. What's bugging me is the fact he's doing all our work for us. I'm beginning to feel like a fraud. I mean, we don't even pay him, do we?'

Norman worked his mouth a couple of times, but nothing came out. It was a good thirty seconds before he could think of anything to say.

'You know, I never thought of it like that,' he said, quietly.

'But you get what I mean, right?'

'Yeah, I do. I got lazy somewhere along the line, didn't I?'

'It's not just you, Norm. I'm here, too. I think we both got lazy because using Vinnie is easy. The problem is we're now relying on him, but I don't think it's right.'

'What about Stella?' asked Norman. 'Haven't we been relying on her as well?'

'Well, yeah,' said Slater guiltily. 'I've been thinking about that, too.'

Norman had a sinking feeling.

'You're not going to stop seeing her over this, are you?'

'No, I am not!' said Slater, vehemently.

'I'm glad to hear it,' said a relieved Norman. 'You'd be a bloody fool if you did.'

'That is not going to happen. Anyway, I don't think Stella's going to be able to help us anymore. She won't say for sure, but I get the feeling they're going to pension her off.'

Norman turned to stare at Slater.

'Holy crap! When's that going to happen?'

'I don't know. She won't tell me exactly what's happening. I think she's trying to prove something to herself by handling it all on her own.'

Norman was feeling distinctly uncomfortable, but he knew Slater was right. Initially, Vinnie had helped them because he thought he owed Norman for turning his life around when he was a teenager. He had been only too happy to help as he saw it as a way of showing his gratitude. But that was back then.

'Vinnie must have paid back whatever he felt he owed you by now, hasn't he?' asked Slater.

'Several times over,' admitted Norman, guiltily. 'But he's never complained.'

'Of course, he hasn't,' said Slater. 'I might not like the guy, but when I met him, I saw for myself how much he appreciates what you did for him. He worships you, Norm, and because of that there's no way he can say "no" to you.'

'You think I'm using him?' asked Norman.

'That's not what I mean, and I don't think Vinnie would see it like that. I think he's become a habit for us. We use him like we used to use the tech unit when we were in the police.'

'Now I feel like crap,' said Norman. 'And it doesn't matter what you say; I have been using him, even if it wasn't intentional.'

They drove on in silence for a minute or two.

'Are you okay?' asked Slater.

'Yeah, except I now feel like shite, and I wish I hadn't started this conversation.'

'So what do you want to do about it?' asked Slater.

'You mean Vinnie? I think you're probably right, and we should stop using him.'

'I think it's for the best,' said Slater. 'Maybe we should look into getting a techie on the payroll.'

'We certainly couldn't afford Vinnie, that's for sure,' said Norman. 'He earns more in a week than we make in twelve months.' He thought for a minute. 'I'm getting confused here. Just the other day we were talking about closing down, and now you're talking about taking on someone to handle tech stuff.'

For once Slater seemed to have nothing to say.

'Let's face it, we're in a mess aren't we?' said Norman, unhappily. 'We're making no money and yet here we are talking about a future we can't afford. And, worst of all, neither of us seems to have a solution. I'm not sure we even know what we're trying to do anymore.'

Slater sighed.

'Yeah, you're right,' he said. 'We've got to stop farting around and get real. The first thing we need to do is see if we have a realistic chance of finding any work. If that ever happens, we'll work out what we can afford. We're going to need equipment as well.'

'Right then,' said Slater. 'Let's put this doom and gloom shit to one side and focus on what we're supposed to be doing. We can come back to this later.'

'Amen to that,' said Norman.

13

They entered East Winton from the north. It was a small village well off the beaten track with a collection of very old, and very new, houses, all gathered around the central feature of the village green which was big enough to be home to a cricket pitch. Also situated around the green were an ancient church and an equally old pub.

'That looks like a nice old pub,' said Norman, as they passed by.

'We can have lunch there later and see if it's as nice on the inside,' said Slater.

There were very few houses after the green, and they were through the village and leaving to the south before they knew it.

'Now that's what I call a small village,' said Norman. 'Blink, and you would have missed it.'

His phone beeped to indicate a text message.

'Crap,' he said. 'Vinnie says the phone is still switched off. He's going to keep monitoring, but he says he has no idea where it is now.'

'Oh well, I suppose it was too much to hope the person was going to wait for us to come and catch them,' said Slater.

'Yeah, I guess so. Still, we're here now, so we might as well take a look around.'

'This bend up ahead must be where Lilly lost control,' said Slater.

He eased the car into the bend and was surprised to find a lay-by off to the left. A bank of soil had been built up between the road and the lay-by, so it was hidden, apart from the entrance.

'That's handy,' he said, steering the car off the road, into the lay-by and then coming to a halt. 'We'll stop here and have a nose around.'

They climbed from the car and took a look at their surroundings. As Vinnie's map had indicated, the area either side of the road was merely grass, and trees. The trees were bereft of leaves at this time of the year so they could see much further than they would have been able to if they were in full leaf. But there was no sign of anyone, walking a dog or otherwise.

The only thing of note was an old car which had been dumped at the far end of the lay-by.

They wandered back to the road, and following Slater's map, made their way along the verge to the crash site.

'Nothing to see here,' said Norman.

'I'm not surprised. I suppose I was letting optimism get the better of me.'

'There's nothing wrong with optimism,' said Norman, 'but the crash was two years ago.'

They spent ten minutes comparing the site to the map, working out where Lilly must have lost control, and where the car finished up.

'I still can't believe a fourteen-year-old girl could have driven the ten miles from where she's supposed to have stolen the car. According to the police report the car was driven in a big circle starting from Lower Winton heading east. At the time she crashed they think she was heading back, presumably to return the car to the Crothers' garage. That means she drove through the outskirts of Winchester, and then two other villages, only to lose control here. That doesn't sound right to me.'

'You know, when you put it like that, it is hard to believe,' said Norman. 'But then, maybe by the time she got here she was getting over-confident, or tired. It is the sort of bend where you could easily lose control.'

He looked at Slater.

'You're not convinced, are you?'

'I just don't get it,' said Slater. 'If she had just stolen the car and only gone a short distance, I might be persuaded, but it makes no sense like this. If she had driven this far, I think she would have got a feel for it. That would make her less likely to have an accident wouldn't it?'

'Come on,' said Norman. 'Let's get some lunch, then this afternoon we'll have another look through what we know. Maybe we'll find something to convince you.'

Slater grunted moodily but followed Norman back to the car.

'Am I seeing things?' asked Norman. He pointed at the abandoned car, sixty yards away, at the other end of the lay-by.

What appeared to be a faint wisp of smoke rose from behind it.

'Looks like it's on fire,' said Slater. 'Come on; we'd better take a look.'

As they walked cautiously towards the car, it became clear the fire was just beyond it. They slowed as they reached the car, and peered inside. A couple of blankets and a few meagre possessions suggested it could even be someone's home. They crept down the side of the car until they could see beyond it. A small fire was burning in a makeshift brazier a few feet from the back end and, before it, a man perched on an upturned bucket, trying to absorb the feeble warmth emitting from it.

'Morning,' said Norman, cheerfully.

Startled, the man swung around and gave them a baleful look.

'I'm doing nothin' wrong,' he said. 'Just trying' to keep warm.'

'Hey, no problem,' said Norman. 'We thought the car was on fire, so we came to take a look.'

'Well, it's not on fire, so you can piss off.'

If he thought his belligerence was going to put Norman off, he was soon disappointed.

'You live here, huh?' asked Norman.

'What do you think?'

'I think you must get pretty cold, especially at night. I'm wondering how you manage to keep warm?'

'Nosey bastard, ain't you?'

'Have you lived here long?'

'What is this? Mastermind?'

'I'm just trying to be friendly,' said Norman.

'I don't need friends.'

Norman said nothing. With any luck, the man would feel he had to fill the silence. Sure enough...

'I've been here three years,' he said, 'not that it's any of your business.'

'I suppose you were here when the accident happened?'

'What accident?'

'Young girl,' said Norman, pointing vaguely in the direction of the road. 'She stole a sports car, lost control on the bend over there, and died in the crash.'

'Oh, that. Yeah, I was here.'

'Did you see what happened?'

'Can't see from here, because of that bank.'

He nodded towards the bank of soil that separated the road and the lay-by. It was about six feet high.

'You'd have a good view from up top there,' suggested Norman.

'What if I did?'

'I'm just curious that's all.'

'Well, I've got nothing to say. The police didn't ask me about it, so why should you?'

'Okay, fair enough,' said Norman.

The man turned away from them, returning his attention to trying to keep warm, and they stood in silence contemplating his back for a minute or two.

'When did you last have a square meal?' asked Norman.

'What d'you care?'

'I've been hungry,' said Norman. 'I know what it's like.'

The man turned again, looked Norman up and down, then spat on the ground.

'I doubt if you've got the faintest idea what it's like.'

He turned back to the fire and raised his hands to warm them.

'Okay, you're right. I've never had to live rough,' admitted Norman, sheepishly. 'But we'd like to help. Can we buy you some food?'

The man scratched his nose.

'I can't stop you if that's what you want to do.'

'We'll be back later,' said Norman. 'You just wait here.'

The man spun around to stare at Norman as if he were mad.

'Where else am I going to be?'

'Yeah, right,' said Norman. 'I'm sorry. That was a stupid thing to say.'

The man watched, scowling, as they walked back to their car. When he was satisfied they were going, he turned back to his fire, reaching forward to throw on another piece of the wood he had collected from the surrounding woodland.

'So, if he was here when Lilly crashed the car,' said Norman, as they climbed into the car, 'D'you think he saw anything?'

'I think it would have been hard for him to ignore it if he heard the crash,' said Slater. He looked towards the road. 'Mind you, he's right about that bank, but if he climbed up...'

'Yeah, he didn't deny it did he?'

'He's a confrontational bugger. He's not looking to do anyone any favours.'

'D'you think we can win him over?'

'It's worth a try,' said Slater. 'Although I'm not so sure we'll gain much by it.'

'At the very least you'll get that warm, fuzzy, feeling from helping someone worse off than you,' said Norman.

Slater started the car.

'Yeah, I suppose I will,' he said.

'I wonder where the nearest shop is,' said Norman.

'It's not in East Winton, that's for sure.'

'How does a guy like that survive, all the way out here?' asked Norman. 'I get that he lives in the car, but he has to eat. What does he do for food? And what about water? I mean, I can see personal hygiene isn't at the top of his list, but everybody has to drink, don't they?"

'He must exist on handouts,' suggested Slater. 'It's not as if he can walk to the local shop, is it? And even if he could, I doubt he has any money.'

Norman sighed.

'It's not right, you know. Doesn't it make you feel uncomfortable?'

'Well, yeah,' admitted Slater, 'but perhaps he chooses to live this way for a reason.'

'Oh, come on. No-one chooses to live in a car dumped in a lay-by.'

'Apparently, this guy does,' said Slater. 'And I think he made it clear he didn't take very kindly to you poking your nose into his business.'

'You don't think we should help him?'

'I already agreed we should try, but I think sometimes you have to accept that not everyone wants help, even if you think they need it.'

'I won't sleep tonight if we don't get him some food.'

'We're going to get him some food, right now.'

He turned out of the lay-by, and headed away from East Winton, towards the nearest town and, hopefully, a supermarket.

TWO HOURS later they returned to the lay-by. In the boot of their car, they had several bags containing food, all non-perishable, and various items they thought might be useful to a man living in a car.

'And finally, we got you a couple of bags of these logs that are supposed to last for hours,' said Norman, lifting the last of the shopping from the back of the car. 'They're supposed to give out plenty of heat, too.'

The man pointed to his left.

'Put 'em down 'ere where I can reach 'em.'

They had just spent the best part of a hundred quid at the supermarket. Slater didn't resent it; God knows it wasn't exactly going to change the guy's life, but he thought a "thank you" wouldn't go amiss. There again, he had no idea what the ungrateful man's story was, so he resisted the temptation to point it out.

'That should keep you going for a few days,' he said.

The man was sifting through one of the shopping bags. He lifted a container out and wrinkled his nose as he read the label.

'I don't like powdered milk.'

Norman could see the man's lack of gratitude was pushing Slater close to the limit of his patience

'It's not my favourite, either,' he admitted, hastily, 'but fresh milk won't keep without a fridge.'

The man grunted his reluctant acceptance of this fact.

'Yeah. I suppose you're right.'

Then he jumped visibly at the sound as a car suddenly pulled into the lay-by. He peered cautiously from behind his vehicle, then visibly relaxed as the car drove across to where they were, and pulled up. A bearded man wearing jeans and a large coat jumped out, carrying a small parcel wrapped in foil. He regarded Slater and Norman with suspicion.

'Everything all right, Tim?' he called out.

The man, grunted as he settled back in front of his fire.

The newcomer walked across to join them.

'Bacon Rolls,' he said, handing over the foil package.

'Is there a problem?' the newcomer asked, turning to the two detectives.

'Not at all. We just brought him some food, and dry logs,' said Norman.

'Why?'

'We're just doing the guy a favour,' added Slater.

'What do you want from him?'

Slater thought about lying, then thought better of it.

'Actually, we're private investigators. We're looking for a missing boy, and the trail led us here.'

'You surely don't think Tim has anything to do with it?'

'Of course not. It's just that the boy's girlfriend crashed a car on the bend over there a couple of years ago. We think it might have some bearing on why he went missing. We just wanted to know if Tim saw anything that might help us.'

'Can I speak with you guys?'

'Sure,' said Norman.

The man led them away from Tim. When he was happy they were out of earshot he stopped.

'Who are you?'

Norman extended his hand.

'I'm Norman Norman, and this is my partner, Dave Slater.'

'I'm Kelly Sellars,' said the man as he shook their hands.

'And you look out for Tim, is that it?' asked Norman.

'I do what I can for him, but he doesn't like to accept charity. I make sure he doesn't go hungry. You haven't bought him any booze have you?'

'No way,' said Norman. 'We wouldn't buy anyone booze no matter who they were.'

'Thank goodness for that.'

'He has a problem, right?' asked Slater.

'He's an alcoholic, but he's been clean for quite a while now. That's one of the reasons he lives out here. He's banned from the pub, and he has no money, so there's no temptation.'

'Well, I can assure you we won't be tempting him,' insisted Norman.

'I sincerely hope not,' said Sellars. 'Even so, I'm not happy about you trying to buy him with gifts.'

'We're not trying to buy him,' said Norman. 'It's a gesture of goodwill.'

'We're not going to take it all back if he refuses to speak to us,' explained Slater.

'Even so, I don't want you upsetting him,' said Sellars.

'We're not trying to upset him,' said Norman.

'It'll help to know his name's Tim,' said Slater.

'That's not his real name,' said Sellars.

'Oh? So what is his real name?'

'He says it doesn't matter. He wants to be called Tim. He says most people would prefer him to be invisible, so that's what he is. T.I.M. The Invisible Man.'

'Jeez, I never thought of it like that,' said Norman, 'but I guess I understand where he's coming from.'

'Do you know how he came to be here?' asked Slater.

'From what I can make out he's ex-forces. Got blown up in Afghanistan. They said he was lucky to get away with no physical damage, other than a few scratches, but that ignores the mental scars he carries with him all the time.'

'PTSD?' asked Norman.

'Yes, that's right.'

'Shit,' said Slater. 'I had no idea.'

'Yes, well, that's half the problem, isn't it?' said Sellars. 'People don't know, but they still judge. To most people, Tim's just some waste of space down and out, who chooses to live in an old car when, in reality, he's a bloody hero!'

Slater felt appropriately humbled.

'Is there nowhere he can stay?' he asked.

'He likes it out here because it's pretty quiet most of the time, and with all these trees he has plenty of cover if he feels the need to run and hide.'

'You seem to know a lot about him,' said Norman. 'Have you been looking after him long?'

'Ever since he arrived three years ago. I live in the village back there. I've asked him to come and stay with me, but he won't have it. He says he doesn't feel safe in a building. Don't forget, in his head he's still fighting a war. Out here he can see the enemy coming.'

'He didn't run from us,' said Slater.

'I bet he saw you coming. If he didn't run, it means he didn't see you as a threat.'

'Do you know if he was here the night the girl died in a car crash?'

'Yes, he was here. I remember he told me about it.'

'Did he see anything?'

'The only thing Tim said was when he heard the crash he thought he was back in Afghanistan. I assumed that meant he ran for his life into the trees, so I doubt he would have seen much.'

'D'you think he would speak to us about it?'

'I don't know about that.'

'Could you ask him?' pleaded Norman. 'If he says no, then fair enough we'll leave him alone.'

Sellars seemed to be weighing things up.

'Wait here,' he said after a short deliberation. 'I'll go and ask him.'

'How small do I feel now?' muttered Norman as they watched Sellars make his way over to Tim.

'Yeah. I would have liked the earth to open up and swallow me, too,' said Slater. 'Kelly Sellars sure has a passion for war heroes. It makes you wonder if there's more to it than meets the eye.'

Norman looked surprised.

'You think that was fake?'

'No, not at all. I was thinking the opposite. He's way too real to be faking.'

Sellars was heading back towards them.

'Tim says he will speak with you, but he doesn't feel up to it just now. He's just eaten. He always feels like crap for an hour or two after.'

'He should see a doctor,' suggested Norman.

'Yes, he should,' said Sellars, with a grim smile, 'and don't think I haven't told him so. The thing is he doesn't have much time for the medical profession.'

'Did he say when we should come back?'

'How about Monday morning, say about 10 o'clock?'

'Yeah, no problem,' said Norman.

Sellars handed him a card.

'Call me when you're on the way. I'll make sure he's here, and I'll sit with him.'

'You want to be here, too?' asked Norman.

'He'll be more comfortable if he's not outnumbered. That's not a problem, is it?'

'No, I guess not' said Slater. 'It makes perfect sense now we know his situation.'

14

It was a grey, chilly, Saturday morning, but Slater was in a good mood. He had just collected Stella and her mother's dog, and they were going to spend the morning walking.

'I just want to take a little diversion,' he told Stella.

'Where, and why?'

'I need to speak to a boy called Lewis. He works in the cafe on his father's farm on Saturdays.'

'This is to do with your secret case, isn't it?'

'It's not a secret case, now you're already involved, is it?' said Slater. 'I just don't want you getting in any deeper.'

'I hope you're not going to suggest I should sit in the car and wait.'

'No, of course not.'

'But won't that let me in on more of the secret?'

Slater could see the beginnings of a grin on her face.

'You're right,' he said. 'Perhaps you should sit in the car and wait.'

Her head snapped round to stare at him, but now she could see the grin on his face.

'Ha! You wouldn't dare,' she said, and he laughed with her.

'How long will it take?' she asked. 'I don't like leaving the dog in the back of the car.'

'No more than twenty minutes. And it's not exactly a hot day is it? I'm sure the dog won't mind.'

'Does this mean I get a hot chocolate before our walk?'

'Is that a big enough bribe?'

She smiled happily.

'On this occasion, yes.'

They drove on for minute or two, then Slater spoke.

'So, how did the interview go?' he asked.

The smile disappeared from her face, and Slater felt the atmosphere in the car turn distinctly chilly.

'No better than I expected,' she said, grimly.

'What does that mean?'

'I'd rather not talk about it.'

He glanced in her direction, but her eyes were glued to the road ahead.

'Are you serious?' he asked.

'Yes, perfectly,' she said, tersely. 'Which part of "I'd rather not talk about it" are you having trouble understanding?'

'Hey! Easy,' he said. 'Don't bite my head off. I'm not looking for a fight, I'm just interested, that's all. I'm on your side, you know.'

'Sorry,' she said, contritely. 'I know you're only trying to help, but I'm not ready to talk about it just yet. Maybe later.'

Slater knew this was a career-defining moment for Stella, and he understood she needed time to think about whatever had been discussed.

'Okay,' he said. 'Whatever you say. I'll try to mind my own business.'

'Thank you.'

In a rare show of familiarity, she reached across, rested a hand on his thigh, and gave it a little pat. Slater glanced down. It was only a small gesture of affection, but this was a big deal in their relationship, and he understood what it meant for both of them.

. . .

Lewis Godden was a fresh-faced 16-year-old who worked on his parents' farm at weekends and during school holidays. Like many farmers, the Goddens had a shop on the farm selling their own produce, and a cafe providing coffee, cakes, and snacks. This particular Saturday, Lewis was working tables in the cafe. It was still early, and the place was quiet, so Slater and Stella had to watch through the window for a couple of minutes to work out which tables Lewis was looking after.

Satisfied they would get an opportunity to speak to him, they made their way over to a corner table, took their seats and perused the menu. They didn't have to wait long.

'Good morning,' said Lewis, pleasantly. 'Are you ready to order?'

Stella smiled up at Lewis.

'I'll have a hot chocolate, please.'

Lewis turned to Slater.

'And you, sir?'

'I'll have the same, please.'

Lewis gave them a bright smile and headed off to make their drinks. A couple of minutes later he was back, carefully placing Stella's mug on the table first, and then Slater's.

Slater smiled back.

'You're Lewis, right?' he asked.

'Yes, that's right.'

'Can I speak to you for a couple of minutes?'

Lewis looked around uncertainly.

'You're not in any trouble,' Slater assured him. 'Trust me, this won't take long, and you're not busy in here yet.'

'What's it about?'

'Mickey Crothers.'

Lewis licked his lips and glanced around the room, but there was no sign of his boss.

'Okay, but please be quick. My parents might own the farm, but as far as work's concerned, I'm the same as everyone else here.'

'So you are friends with Mickey Crothers?'

'Er, yeah,' said Lewis, hesitantly.

'I heard you were his best mate.'

'I like to think so. Is that a problem?'

'No, of course not,' said Slater. 'It's just that he's missing, and his mother's asked me to find him.'

'He's not missing. He's with his father.

'D'you know that for sure?'

'He sent me a text saying he was. He wants to spend some time with his dad. Is that a crime?'

'Of course not, but his mother doesn't know where he is, and she's worried about him.'

'That's her fault. Maybe if she hadn't tried to keep Mickey away from his dad, he wouldn't have run off like that. He will come back, you know. He's got exams coming up next term; he won't want to mess them up.'

'D'you known where his father lives?'

Lewis shook his head.

'Even Mickey didn't know until a few days ago.'

'But he didn't tell you?'

'No way!'

'He didn't trust you?'

'I don't think it was that. Mickey said his dad wanted to keep it a secret, and he was worried his mother would start hassling me for the address. He said if I didn't know, I couldn't be bullied into telling anyone.'

He looked defiantly at Slater, who smiled back at him.

'Okay, Lewis, point taken,' he said. 'Has he been in touch with his father for long?'

'They sometimes kept in touch by text, but his mum never knew.'

'So, why didn't he go and see him before?'

'He never even mentioned wanting to go and see him before, but then a couple of weeks ago he told me he was going to go, but that I shouldn't tell anyone.'

'But why go now?'

'I don't know. Maybe Mickey waited until he was sixteen so his mother wouldn't be able to force him to come back.'

Lewis was looking at his boss, who was hovering behind the counter, keeping an eye on him.

'I have to go,' he said.

'What can you tell me about Mickey and Lilly Becker?' said Slater. 'She was his girlfriend, wasn't she?'

'I wouldn't exactly put it like that. They grew up together, but they were more like brother and sister than boyfriend and girlfriend. He was upset when she died.'

'He didn't think she had betrayed his trust when she stole the car?'

'Mickey didn't believe she stole that car, and he still doesn't believe it.'

'Really? Why does he think that?'

'I don't know why, I just know he does.' He looked nervously at his boss, once again. 'Look I'm going to have to go.'

Slater smiled at him, again.

'Okay Lewis, thank you for your help.'

They watched as the boy rushed off, apologising to his boss as he got near her.

'What do you think?' Slater asked Stella.

She raised her eyebrows.

'You're going to involve me now?'

'I just want a second opinion.'

'He seems like a nice enough kid.'

'Yeah, but does he know where Mickey is?'

'I don't think so. In my opinion Lewis was telling the truth about that.'

'You think he was lying about something else?'

'Not so much lying, as not telling you everything.'

'Yeah, I thought so, too,' said Slater. 'But, unlike you, I'm not convinced he doesn't know where Mickey is. Wouldn't you tell your best mate where you were going?'

Stella was raising her drink to her lips, but she stopped and pulled a face.

'Maybe not, if I thought my mum was going to try to find out where I was, and it would put my best mate in a difficult position. As Lewis said, he can't tell what he doesn't know, can he?'

'Okay, but why is it so important Mickey keeps it a secret? I mean he's sixteen now so his mother can't make him come home even if she knows where his father lives.'

'Lewis said it was his father who wanted it kept secret. Maybe he thinks his ex-wife is a danger. You never know, she could have threatened to ruin his life. Don't forget, "hell hath no fury", and all that jazz.'

'Yeah, maybe,' said Slater, thoughtfully, 'but I doubt it. I'm pretty sure he's the golden goose who enables her lifestyle. If she sinks him, she sinks herself as well.'

'Maybe she doesn't care about that.'

'I've met her, Stella. I'm sure she hates him enough to want to destroy him, but she's very protective of her son. I can't believe she would want to destroy herself, and Mickey, in the process.'

Stella had no response to that.

'I just can't help wondering, why would he choose to go now?' said Slater. 'Lewis tells us Mickey's been in touch with his father all along, and suddenly, now, he decides to go and see him. Why? There must be a reason!'

'Perhaps Lewis is right, and he was waiting until he turned sixteen so his mother couldn't make him come back. Perhaps it's that simple.'

'Mmm, maybe,' said Slater.

'You're not convinced, are you?' she asked.

'Not really, no.'

She smiled.

'It's no good sitting there, brooding,' she said. 'You need something to take your mind off it. I find walking the dog works for me, and she must be bored sitting in the back of the car.'

'Yeah, you're right. She'll be well bored by now, but at least it's not a hot day.'

'I wouldn't have brought her along if it had been.'

'No, of course not. That wouldn't be fair,' agreed Slater.

'We can take her back home to Mum's afterwards, and then I'll buy you lunch.'

'Now that sounds like a plan,' said Slater. 'Let's go!'

15

Sellars raised a hand in greeting as they turned into the lay-by on Monday morning, and then indicated he wanted them to park next to his car. Forty yards away they could see smoke slowly spiralling skywards from behind the old car.

'Tim prefers it if we approach on foot rather than driving up and surrounding him,' explained Sellars, as they climbed from their car. 'Cars spook him. This way he has plenty of time to see who's coming.'

'Does he get a lot of trouble out here?' asked Norman.

'He's had trouble once or twice in the past, but not recently. Most of the people who stop here are from the village bringing food and stuff, and they're all respectful of his situation and his needs.'

'They don't try to evict him?' asked Slater. 'Some people would object to a homeless guy living so close to their village.'

'He seems to be far enough out of the village to avoid that sort of snobbery. The people who object don't have to see him, and those who feel sympathy try to understand and help him get by.'

'So, mostly he's left in peace? I suppose that's something,' said Slater.

'I'd be grateful if you're mindful of that fact, and try not to upset him,' said Sellars, as he began to lead them towards Tim's car.

'As we told you the other day, we're not trying to upset anyone,' said Norman. 'We just want to know if he saw anything that might be relevant to our investigation.'

Once again Tim was sitting before his makeshift brazier, trying to absorb as much warmth as he could. Norman noticed he was now wearing the same enormous coat Sellars had been wearing on Saturday.

'Good morning Tim,' called Sellars as they approached. 'These are the two detectives you agreed to meet. Do you remember them?'

Tim turned and gave them a hostile look, his jaw jutting forward.

'Of course, I remember,' he said, scathingly. 'There's nothing wrong with my memory. That's the whole essence of my problem, isn't it?'

'Morning Tim,' said Norman. 'How are you, today?'

'Same as I was yesterday, and the day before that.'

'Look,' said Norman. 'We're not going to insult you by pretending we understand your situation. I believe it's one of those cases where you had to be there, and neither of us has.'

'Is there a point to this speech?'

'Yeah, there is,' said Slater. 'What we're trying to say is we're not here to score points, or to try to catch you out. We're just looking for a sixteen-year-old boy, and you might know something that could help us.'

'How long has this boy been missing?' asked Tim.

'Technically he's not missing. We know he's with his father, but we don't know where he is.'

'How old did you say he was?'

'Sixteen.'

Tim frowned.

'The accident was two years ago. The boy would have been fourteen back then. How is what happened back then going to be relevant to where he is now?'

'We're not sure,' said Slater. 'Maybe you're right, and it's not, but the girl who died was his girlfriend, so we have to consider the possibility.'

Tim turned back to his fire and brooded silently for a minute or so, and then he seemed to sit a little taller as if he'd made a decision.

'I can tell you there was no young boy involved in that accident,' he said, finally, without looking around.

'So you did see it,' said Norman. 'Can you tell us what happened?'

'I didn't see the crash because I was asleep, but I heard it,' said Tim. 'There was this huge crash, and then the screeching of metal as the car slid along the road on its roof.' He turned around a haunted look on his face. 'It took me back, you know? The noise woke me up, and I can tell you, I didn't hang around, I was off into the trees. I've dug myself a hole back there, to protect me. I was up there in a matter of seconds.'

He looked around anxiously as if the memory would invoke an attack from unseen enemies.

'What happened next,' asked Sellars, gently. 'It's all right, you can tell us. You're among friends here.'

Tim looked as if he had suddenly woken from a terrible dream.

'There was this deathly quiet,' he said. 'There always is after an explosion, did you know that?'

He looked from Norman to Slater.

'Yeah, I've heard that,' said Slater.

'What did you do after the crash?' asked Norman.

'It took me a few minutes to realise where I was. Like I say, deathly quiet it was, and then I could hear this sound. At first, I couldn't make out what it was, but it was coming from the direction of the crash. I thought it sounded like someone crying. I was still shaking with the fear, you know, but I thought whoever it was must be hurt, so I made my way back down.

'As I got closer, I was sure I could hear a girl crying. I wanted to help her if I could, so I made my way up the bank.' He pointed to where the bank hiding the lay-by ran alongside the road. 'I crept up and peeped over the top. I was going to see if I could help her, but someone was there already.'

'There was someone at the scene?' asked Slater, astounded. 'Are you sure?'

'Was it the police?' suggested Norman.

'No. They didn't turn up for another twenty minutes or so. I suppose it was lucky they came at all because I don't think anyone called them.'

Norman looked to Slater, who nodded.

'I think it was a routine patrol that found the car,' he said, quietly.

'So, Tim, who was at the car?' asked Norman. 'Was it a man, or a woman? Someone you recognised?'

'It was dark. I couldn't see who it was, but I thought he was there to help the girl, so I didn't need to worry, you know?'

'You said "he",' said Slater. 'Are you sure it was a man?'

Tim seemed to be sorting through a head full of jumbled thoughts looking for the answer.

'I can't be certain, but something must have made me think it was a man.'

'What was he doing?'

'He seemed to be down on his knees leaning inside the car, but I couldn't say for sure.'

'Was he trying to move her?'

'I really couldn't say. Anyway, I could feel myself starting to go by then. I knew I couldn't stay there much longer. The fear was taking over, and I thought I was about to start screaming. I wouldn't have been able to help anyone once that happened, so I ran back to the trench, and I stayed there for the rest of the night.'

'So you have no idea who was by the car, or where they came from?' asked Slater. 'But you think it was probably a man.'

Tim shook his head.

'It's not my fault! He was by the car. I thought he was helping her.'

'It's okay, we're not blaming you,' said Norman. 'Was the girl still crying when you left?'

'I'm pretty sure she had stopped by then.'

Tim was visibly upset by now, his hands shaking, and his eyes wild. Norman looked at Slater who gave the merest nod.

'Hey look, Tim, you've been very helpful,' said Norman. 'I can see just talking about this has upset you, and we're both sorry about that. Let us leave you in peace now. Will you be okay on your own?'

Sellars frowned.

'I'll stay with him,' he said.

'I'm sorry, we upset him,' said Norman.

Sellars sighed.

'Yeah, well, at least I'm here to look after him. I won't leave until he's feeling better.'

'Thanks for helping us,' said Slater. 'It's been beneficial.'

'Bloody hell, Norm,' said Slater, as he started the car. 'If he's telling the truth, and there was someone else in that car, it could mean Lizzie Becker is right, and her daughter isn't a car thief. I said I couldn't see how Lilly could have been driving that car when she couldn't reach the pedals!'

'Hold on a minute,' said Norman. 'Let's not get ahead of ourselves. We've only got the word of a deeply traumatised man who arrived after the accident. Even if he did see someone, it doesn't mean they were in the car with Lilly when it crashed.'

Slater had been just about to pull away, but now he sat back in his seat and turned to Norman, his eyes wide.

'What do you mean "if" he saw someone?'

'The guy just told us he was falling apart after he heard the crash.' explained Norman. 'How do we know he wasn't hallucinating? Maybe he was reliving something that happened to him in Afghanistan.'

'Yeah, fine,' said Slater, 'but what if wasn't hallucinating, and he did see someone?'

'It still doesn't mean they were in the car. Like you said before, someone could have come upon the accident and stopped, but they were too late to do anything to help.'

'So, why didn't they call the police?'

'Because they had stolen Lilly's phone?' suggested Norman. 'Or, because they panicked?'

But Slater wasn't listening.

'But the guy was on his knees leaning inside the car,' he insisted.

'Maybe he was trying to help her.'

'Or, maybe he was moving her so it would look like she was driving!'

'We can't say that,' argued Norman. 'We have no proof!'

'But what other reason could there be for moving Lilly and then disappearing before the police arrive? Think about it. This adds up. I've been telling you all along that it didn't make sense for her to be on her own.'

Norman turned a stare in Slater's direction.

'What?' asked Slater.

'You're the one who keeps telling me we can't afford to take on cases that don't pay their way. We're only supposed to be finding Mickey Crothers so he can help us find out who sent the text message to Lizzie Becker, right? That's what we're being paid for.'

'Yeah, but it's not as if Mickey's in any danger, is it? We know he's with his father, and we know he's safe. We just don't know exactly where they are.'

'We don't know he's safe, we think he's safe,' said Norman. 'We're not going to know for sure until we find his father. Besides, Lizzie Becker didn't ask us to investigate the accident. She just asked us to find out who sent that damned text.'

'Yes, but she doesn't believe Lilly stole that car, and like I say, what if Tim did see someone?'

'I think it's a very big "if",' argued Norman.

'Are you telling me you think we should ignore the possibility that Lilly Becker was innocent? I've had a hunch about this right from the start.'

'You and your hunches. I'm just saying—'

'Come on, Norm. She was just fourteen years old when she died. She was branded a car thief without a chance to defend herself. You were on about warm, fuzzy feelings the other day. You'd get that same feeling with bells on if we proved she was innocent.'

Norman turned to face the front, shaking his head.

'You're unbelievable, d'you know that?' he said. 'We were talking about taking on a techie earlier. How are we going to pay for something like that if we're going to work for nothing all the time?'

But Slater had the bit between his teeth now.

'But look at it the other way,' he insisted. 'Think of the publicity we would get if we proved Lilly was innocent!'

'We don't seem to have benefited from publicity before.'

'We'd have people queueing at the door.'

'And we'll be broke if we can't prove it.'

'Huh! That's a good one. We're already broke if you're going to worry about that,' said Slater.

'As I said, publicity never helped us before,' said Norman.

'That's because we didn't know how to make it work for us. This time we'll get some help.'

'You mean you know someone in PR who works for nothing? Well, I hope so because that's what we'll need.'

Slater studied the side of Norman's face, but Norman refused to turn and look at him.

'What if what Tim saw was a cover-up? What if he saw the driver dragging Lilly's body across to the driver's side before he made his escape?' urged Slater, but Norman continued to stare out of the windscreen at nothing in particular.

'I can't believe you don't accept there's a possibility someone else could have been in that car, Norm, and I can't believe you don't want to find out what really happened.'

Norman rubbed his face and groaned.

'Jeez, you can be the most contrary bugger sometimes, you know that?' he said, turning to look at Slater.

Slater winked and gave him a wry smile.

'Yeah, but you wouldn't want me to be predictable and boring, would you?'

Now Norman smiled, too. 'You're an arsehole. You know that don't you?'

'Of course, I do. It's just one of the many reasons you love working with me, right?'

'And arrogant, too,' said Norman.

'C'mon, Norm, be honest. You know you want to do this as much as I do.'

Norman shook his head, but he couldn't shake off the smile.

'Okay, okay. We'll take a look at the possibility.'

'Now that sounds much more like my favourite optimist speaking,' said Slater.

'But we're not going to stop looking for Mickey, or finding out who sent that text,' insisted Norman.

'Definitely not,' said Slater. 'We've got even more reason to find Mickey now.'

'Oh, and you're buying lunch,' said Norman.

Slater put the car in gear.

'I wouldn't have it any other way, Norm,' he said.

An hour later, having eaten an excellent, if expensive, lunch in the "nice old pub" Norman had spotted in East Winton they were heading back to their office.

'I'm tempted to go back and speak to Mia Crothers again,' said Slater.

'Any particular reason?'

'Yeah, she was so damned dismissive of Lilly and so sure she stole that car I'd like to tell her she's got it all wrong.'

'This has really got to you, hasn't it?' asked Norman.

'I can't stop thinking about how upset Lizzie Becker was, and how she was so adamant her daughter wasn't a car thief, but no-one would listen. It just seems so unfair that the poor kid was buried with that label when it's simply not true. I feel it's down to us to put the record straight.'

Norman nodded. 'Yeah, I kinda thought that's what it was, but don't forget this is still speculation. We don't have any convincing evidence to prove you're right.'

'Mia Crothers had known Lilly since she was a baby. I feel she should have had a bit of faith in her and not dismissed her so quickly.

It's not right.'

'Okay, okay,' said Norman, gently. 'I get the point, but I don't think you should go anywhere near Mia Crothers until you've at least cooled off a bit, and if you want my support on this, I'm going to have to insist. Is that a deal?'

'I can't shake your hand while I'm driving.'

'I think, after all this time, I can accept your word without the handshake.'

'Okay. We have a deal.'

'Good,' said Norman.

'Do you think we should tell Lizzie Becker about our suspicions?' asked Slater.

'Honestly? Let's wait. It wouldn't do to raise her hopes and then find we're wrong, or we can't prove it.'

'Fair enough. So what's our next move?'

'We still haven't got any closer to finding Jason and Mickey Crothers,' said Norman. 'As you said before lunch, we need to speak to Mickey. Tim says there was no young boy there, but it was dark, right?'

'You think Mickey might have been in the car?'

'Seriously? I think it's highly unlikely,' said Norman, 'but we need to be sure.'

'His mother said he was with her.'

'Yeah, I know, but I want to know what he has to say.'

'I'll have another go at finding Jason this afternoon,' said Slater.

'Okay. I'm going to see what I can find out about our friend Tim,' said Norman. 'I need to understand if he's stable enough to be a reliable witness.'

16

It was 4 pm. For the last two hours, Slater and Norman had each been hunched over a laptop, searching for information on their respective targets.

'I had to take a break,' said Norman, entering Slater's office carrying two mugs of tea. 'My eyes were starting to hurt.'

Slater leaned back in his chair and spun it round to face Norman. He yawned extravagantly, stretched his arms, and then placed his hands behind his head. 'Yeah, I know what you mean, and sitting in this chair for so long does nothing for my back.'

Norman eased past Slater and put the two mugs of tea down on his desk.

'Have you found anything interesting?'

'Not really,' said Slater. 'We already knew Jason worked for Keeling Security. Apart from that, he seems to have kept a pretty low profile. I can't find any trace of him after he left his wife.'

'Not much help, then?'

'I did find a couple of posts on an obscure security industry website that suggested there was some suspicion about the way Keeling Security finds new clients. In both cases, Jason Crothers was mentioned. He had got in touch with a homeowner within a few days of them having their house broken into.'

'Were they asking, how did he know?' asked Norman. 'I expect he has a contact in an Insurance company.'

'Yeah, someone suggested that in the comments,' said Slater, 'but it turns out both these guys were using different Insurers.'

'Maybe he has contacts in every Insurance company.'

'Yeah, that wouldn't surprise me,' agreed Slater. 'So, I suppose what I'm saying is I've got no further forward. What we need is for someone at Keeling to volunteer some information.'

'Not much chance of that if Malcolm Keeling keeps them all on a tight leash.'

Slater yawned again. 'Yeah, but I don't see any other way of finding the guy right now. We don't even have a mobile phone number we can use to track him...' For a moment he stopped talking, and then he sat up straight, suddenly wide awake. 'Jesus, what a bloody fool I am. If we can get Mickey's number we can ask Vinnie to track his phone, and if he's with his dad...'

'Just a couple of things,' said Norman. 'One, we don't have his number, and two, I thought we decided we aren't going to use Vinnie any more.'

Slater slumped back in his chair.

'Shit! Yeah, you're right. Or, did we say we wouldn't use him anymore, after this case?'

'Without Mickey's mobile number it doesn't matter.'

'I'll find it.'

'From where? I seem to recall his mother was adamant she wouldn't part with any information related to Mickey.'

'Okay, so I'll ask Lewis Godden,' said Slater. 'He's Mickey's best mate. He must know his number.'

Norman looked sceptical.

'He's a good kid, and I didn't piss him off,' said Slater. 'If I approach him right, I'm sure he'll help.'

'Yeah, well, good luck with that.'

Slater was convinced, even if Norman remained doubtful.

'Trust me, it'll be fine,' he said, confidently. Then, changing the subject, 'Anyway, it's your turn. How did you get on with Tim? Somehow I can't see him having an extensive social media profile to help you.'

Norman sipped at his tea and looked over the top of his mug at Slater. A sly grin began to take over his face as he placed the mug back on the desk.

'Well, it just so happens one of us is much better at this internet search thing than you.'

'No way,' said Slater. 'You mean you found him? An anonymous guy living in a car?'

'Ah, yes, but the thing about living in a car, even if you're anonymous, is it can give you celebrity status.'

'What?'

'There's a website devoted to the guy!'

'How does that work? I thought he had dropped out of society.'

'I get the impression he probably knows absolutely nothing about the website,' said Norman. 'It just gives a bit of background about why he's there and what his story is.'

'Does it tell us anything we don't know?'

'It seems to say a lot without being specific about anything much, but there's nothing we don't already know. It's been created as a sort of fundraiser. People can contribute to help keep him fed, and to provide blankets and stuff.'

'Who's behind it?'

'Who d'you think is behind it?'

'My guess would be that guy who looks out for him, Kelly Sellars.'

'That's what I thought at first,' said Norman. 'But I'm pretty sure it's not him.'

'So, who is it?'

'I think it might be Mickey.'

Slater nearly fell off his chair.

'What? Mickey Crothers?'

'That's the one.'

'What makes you think that?'

'Because if you follow the links from the website, they go to a 'Just Give' page set up to receive contributions for Tim. None other than Mickey Crothers created the page.'

'No shit! How the hell does sixteen-year-old Mickey know an ex-soldier like Tim? How did they meet?'

'It makes you wonder doesn't it?' said Norman. 'But don't forget East Winton is only a couple of miles from Lower Winton. It's possible their paths could have crossed.'

'I suppose so, but there must be more to it than that. What's the real connection?'

'I thought maybe you might have found some reference to Jason Crothers having been in the Army at some stage. That would have tied it all up quite nicely.'

'I didn't look specifically,' said Slater, 'but it didn't come up anywhere I could see. Do we know what Tim's regiment was? If I know that I can check if Jason was in there, too.'

'Ah, yes, Tim and the Army,' said Norman. 'You need a surname to check out that sort of thing.'

'Oh yeah, of course. We have no idea who Tim is, do we?'

'Well, perhaps we do,' said Norman. 'You see, when I first found the website, like you, I immediately thought of Kelly Sellars, so I checked him out. It turns out he has an older brother called Harvey.'

'Really? And you think Harvey is Tim? Was he ever in the Army?'

'If only. That would have made it all very neat and tidy, wouldn't it? Unfortunately, Harvey has never been in the Army.'

'Crap! It can't be him then.'

'Not so fast,' said Norman. 'Forget about the Army for a minute and listen to this; Harvey had a serious drink problem, got into debt, and lost his job, house, wife, the lot. And he hasn't been officially registered anywhere for over three years, which means he's almost certainly living rough.'

'Unless he's dead.'

Norman sighed.

'Jeez, do you think you could try to be a tad more positive about this? Just focus on what I just said about him being a drunk, a loser, and living rough. Now, does that remind you of anyone we met recently?'

'Well, yeah, of course, it does, but what about the PTSD he brought back from Afghanistan?'

'Admittedly the Army bit doesn't quite fit my hypothesis,' said Norman.

'You can't deny he looks shell-shocked.'

'Yes, but looking isn't the same as being, is it?' argued Norman. 'I think I might look shell-shocked if I lost everything and ended up on the street.'

'You're convinced Tim is Harvey Sellars, aren't you?'

'Let's say I'm more than halfway to being convinced,' admitted Norman. 'Remember when we first came across Kelly Sellars? You said something about him having a passion for war heroes.'

'That's right. I thought Sellars seemed far more protective than he needed to be.'

'Well, maybe he's like that because he's protecting his brother.'

'I see what you mean,' said Slater, thoughtfully. 'But why would he let him live in an old car?'

'If you remember, Kelly did say he'd asked Tim to come and live with him, but Tim refused. Maybe there's bad blood between them.'

'Like what?'

'Jeez, I don't know. How many different reasons can you think of?'

'Okay, what about Tim. Why lie about being in the Army?'

'Perhaps he thinks claiming to be a war hero is better than admitting he's a loser.'

'Isn't there a law against that?'

'He's not wearing a uniform, but claiming former military service to get money would be fraud.'

'Jesus, and to think we bought him all that stuff!'

'Yeah,' said Norman, reasonably, 'but, to be fair, he didn't con us.

He was just a homeless guy we chose to give a helping hand because we wanted to try and win his confidence. At no point did he volunteer any information about the Army. It was Kelly who told us that later. You could even argue that we were trying to con him.'

Slater nodded thoughtfully.

'I guess you're right. I hadn't thought about it like that.'

'But then you also have to ask yourself, is he actually perpetrating a fraud?' asked Norman. 'I mean, he might be spouting bollocks about being in the Army, but if he's unaware of the website, and he's not asking anyone for charity, is he guilty of anything other than being a bullshitter?'

'Ha! That's one for the lawyers to wrangle over,' said Slater.

'It could be the case that Mickey's committing the fraud, even if he's doing it with the best of intentions!'

'Now there's a thought,' said Slater. 'I suppose it would depend on whether he knows the truth.'

'Let's not go any further down that path,' said Norman. 'Whether there is, or isn't, a fraud, and who is committing it, is not our problem. Let someone else waste their time worrying about it.'

'D'you think Mickey's mother knows about Tim, and the website?' asked Slater.

'What difference does it make?'

'I don't know,' said Slater. 'I'm just wondering why he would build the guy a website.'

'Maybe he's just a kind-hearted kid.'

'Possibly,' said Slater. 'Or maybe there's some reason that might be relevant to our case.'

Norman let out a little snort of derision.

'Even if there is a reason, do you seriously think she'd tell us?'

'Probably not, but her reaction might let us know if we should dig a little deeper.'

Norman thought for a second.

'You know, you're right,' he said, decisively. 'It's not always the answer they give that tells you what they know, it's how they react. I think I'm going to go and ask her.'

'What, now?'

'Sure, why not?'

'Can I come?'

'Can I trust you not to bring up the subject of Lilly Becker?'

'I'm not sure I can promise that.'

'In that case, no, you can't come.'

17

It was late afternoon by the time Norman reached Mia Crothers' house. There was a warm glow through the small window in the front door, and other lights in the house and a car on the drive told Norman she must be at home. After the last visit, he was expecting a hostile reception, so he rang the doorbell with a degree of trepidation, and then waited.

A full minute later he was still waiting, so he rang the bell again. He let another minute go by, but still, there was no reply. He wondered should he stay, or should he go. He could think of many reasons why she might not want to answer the door, but years of police experience told him something wasn't right.

He knelt at the door, lifted the flap of the letterbox, and called into the house.

'Mrs Crothers? It's Norman Norman. I called a couple of days ago. I know you probably don't want to speak to me, but I just wanted a quick word. It'll only take a minute, I promise.'

He peered through the letterbox, then put his ear to it and listened hard, hoping to hear a sound that would mean she was okay but choosing to ignore him. He could accept that and leave happy if everything was okay, and his instincts had been wrong. But there was no sound, just an eerie quietness. Again Norman wondered should he stay, or should he go, but a tiny voice nagged away inside his head telling him he couldn't leave without knowing Mia Crothers was okay.

He stepped back and looked up at the house, then crept across to the nearest window and peered inside. The expensively furnished room was lit by a standard lamp behind a comfy looking chair. The room appeared neat and tidy but had the look of being rarely used. A door was open at the far end, and when Norman moved to his left, he found he could see further into the house. Just beyond the door was the hall, and then beyond that, through another door, was what must be the kitchen.

One final step to his left began to narrow his view but allowed him to see just a little further into the kitchen. All he could see, though, was what he assumed to be a pair of Mia's shoes lying on the floor. It seemed odd that the shoes should be there on the floor when the rest of the house looked so tidy but Norman himself wasn't exactly the neatest of people, and he was in no position to criticise someone else for not being perfect.

He took one final look, then headed back to the front door. Then he stopped and went back to the window. He couldn't put his finger on it, but there was something about the way those shoes were lying there, on their sides.

He moved as far across the window as he could, and stared through to the kitchen and the shoes, and now he realised why the shoes didn't look right lying on their sides like that. There were feet inside them. Whoever was in that kitchen was laying on the floor, not moving.

With a turn of speed that he thought he was no longer capable of, Norman rushed around to the back of the house in search of an unlocked door. The kitchen door was the first one he came to, and to his great relief, it was unlocked. He threw the door open and rushed inside to find an ashen Mia Crothers stretched out on the floor.

As he knelt at her side, Norman couldn't miss the unmistakable smell of alcohol emanating from her. He noticed a few small splashes of blood on the floor that had dripped from a small wound to her forehead.

Gently he felt her neck and was relieved to find a good strong pulse. She groaned at his touch, and her eyes flickered open and then closed again.

'Mrs Crothers,' said Norman, softly. 'Are you okay?'

Suddenly her eyes were wide open, and she looked at him in horror.

'What's going on?' she said, panic clear in her voice. 'What are you doing to me?'

She tried to sit up, but Norman didn't think that would be a good idea. As if to confirm his thoughts her eyes began to roll. For a moment he thought she was going to pass out, then he realised she was struggling to try and get his face back in focus.

'Now take it easy, Mrs Crothers,' he said. 'You've banged your head. I'd give it a minute or two before you try to get up.'

She stopped struggling, but she was confused.

'Who are you?' she slurred. 'Why're you in my house?'

Norman silently cursed. It was just his luck to choose to come and interview a drunk.

'My name's Norman. Do you remember me? I'm a detective. I came to see you with my colleague a couple of days ago.'

She looked around, still apparently confused about what was happening, but seemed satisfied with Norman's explanation.

'Has he gone?' she asked.

'Has who gone?'

She stared as if he were the one babbling.

'What? Who? Gone where?' she asked.

Norman sighed. This could turn out to be a long night.

'I just arrived a few minutes ago,' he explained. 'I knocked on the door, but you didn't answer. So I came round the back and found you laying on the floor here.'

'But why would you come round to the back?'

'I just felt something was wrong. I guess it's my old police officer instinct.'

She put her hand to the lump on her forehead, yelped in pain, and then looked at her fingers.

'Blood?' she asked.

Norman nodded. 'You have a lump and a small cut. You must have hit your head when you fell. I should take you to the hospital—'

'No, no, no. I don't need a hospital. Just help me to my feet and get me a glass of brandy. I'll be fine.'

'I'll get you to a chair, but I think maybe you've already had enough to drink.'

'I beg your pardon?' she snapped, eyes blazing.

Norman had touched a nerve. He thought a change of subject might distract her.

'Here, let me help you to your feet.'

He put his arms around her and eased her to her feet.

'Let's get you somewhere more comfortable,' he said.

She pointed to a sturdy pine table with four chairs around it. 'One of those chairs will do just fine.'

Not wishing to irritate her further, Norman did as she asked, settled her onto one of the chairs, and then fetched her a glass of water. She sipped at the water and then glared at him.

'How dare you suggest I'm drunk?' she demanded. 'Whatever makes you think that?'

'Well now, let me see,' said Norman, patiently. 'You were stretched out on the floor with a cut head when I found you, your speech was slurred, you couldn't focus, and even you must be able to smell the booze.'

'I fell and hit my head. Of course, I was a bit woozy for a minute or two, but do I sound drunk now?'

Norman had to concede she wasn't slurring now, and to be fair, she was no more unsteady than could be expected after banging their head.

'Well, no, I can't argue with that,' he admitted, 'but what am I supposed to think with that smell?'

'But it's on the outside.' She pointed to the front of her dress. 'I thought you were a detective! You didn't detect that, did you?'

Norman looked sheepish.

'To be honest, I was more concerned with making sure you were alive,' he said. 'So what happened? Did you spill it?'

Now she did look confused.

'No, he...' She stopped mid-sentence, then began again. 'Yes, that's right. I did. Clumsy of me. I was carrying a small glass of whiskey, and I tripped. It went all over me as I fell. That must have been how I hit my head.'

Norman looked back across the kitchen where he had found her. There was a half-empty bottle of scotch, and an empty glass, on the side. There were a few drops of liquid on the floor, but there was no sign of broken glass anywhere. He turned back to her.

'Lucky you put the glass down before you passed out.'

'What? Oh yes, it was a bit of luck, wasn't it.'

'You know, if I didn't know better, I'd think you weren't quite telling the whole story.'

'I don't know what you mean?'

'Really? You were going to say something about a "he".'

Her ashen face had now flushed a deep red. 'I don't know where that came from. I'm a bit confused. It must be the bang on the head.'

'Yeah, right,' said Norman. 'In that case, maybe I should take you to the hospital.'

'Don't be silly. I'll be fine in a minute.'

'Mrs Crothers, I might look like an idiot, but I was a detective sergeant for many years. I know when someone's not telling me everything.'

'I'm sure I don't know what you mean.'

Norman sighed and shook his head.

'Okay, Mrs Crothers, this is how it's going to go,' he said. 'You can tell me what's going on or I can call the police, and an ambulance.'

'Whatever do we need the police here for?'

'I'm convinced you're not telling me what really happened, so I have to rely on my experience. In my opinion, it's possible someone may have attacked you. If that's the case, for your safety, the police ought to be notified. My conscience wouldn't let me sleep tonight if I didn't take the appropriate action.'

She sighed and rolled her eyes. Norman could see she was close to tears.

'And you really ought to go to the hospital,' he said, gently. 'You hit your head!'

'I'll be fine.'

'Is there someone I can call? You shouldn't be here on your own after a fall like that.'

'Only my son and he's not answering his phone because he'd rather be with his damned father!' she said, bitterly.

She started to get to her feet, but then everything began to spin. Fortunately, Norman was attentive enough to catch her and guide her back onto her chair.

'I think you need to get that head looked at,' said Norman.

'I don't want to spend hours at the hospital on my own,' she said, sadly.

'You won't be on your own,' said Norman. 'I'll take you, wait with you, and then if they give you the all clear I'll bring you home again.'

'I can't ask you to do that.'

'You didn't ask me. Besides, I can't leave you here, can I?'

'You know what hospitals are like. We could be waiting for hours.'

'Maybe we'll get lucky.'

'Don't you have somewhere you should be?'

Norman sighed.

'Yeah, I wish,' he said, wistfully. 'Look, Mrs Crothers, I like to be able to sleep at night. I'll do it a lot better if I'm not worrying about what might have happened to you.'

'I don't know what to say.'

'Just say okay, and tell me where your coat is so I can fetch it for you,' said Norman.

'This is very kind of you,' she said, three hours later, as Norman drove out of the hospital car park.

'No problem, Mrs Crothers,' said Norman. 'The doctor says you're okay, and you tell me you're feeling better. That's the important thing.'

'I think you can stop calling me Mrs Crothers, now,' she said. 'My name is Mia.'

Norman nodded.

'And I'm Norman or Norm.'

'And you don't need to call the police,' she said. 'No-one tried to attack me. I had a shock, that's all.'

'D'you want to tell me about it?'

'It's not... I don't think you can do anything about it.'

'I'm a detective, Mia; you might be surprised how helpful I can be. You mentioned a "he" earlier. Is there a man bothering you?'

'It's a tramp. He came once before, but this afternoon he just suddenly appeared at the back window and frightened me half to death. That's why I fell over and banged my head.'

'What happened to this man?' asked Norman.

'Well, I don't know. He looked as scared as I was, but the next thing I remember, you were there waking me up. Didn't you see him when you arrived?'

'I didn't see anyone,' said Norman. 'I guess he must have run off when he saw you. Can you describe him?'

'He's just a filthy tramp. I suppose he's begging.'

'And you say he came once before?'

'That was several months ago. On that occasion, he came to the front door. I thought he was begging when I opened the door and saw him there. He said he was looking for Jason, that they were old friends.'

'What did you do?'

'I told him Jason doesn't live here anymore and sent him away.'

'Did he tell you his name?'

'No, I don't think he did, but I didn't give him a chance. I found him rather intimidating, and I'm sure he hadn't washed in weeks. He smelled disgusting.'

'And you have no idea why he was looking for Jason?'

'He didn't say why, just that they were old friends.'

'Has this man tried to contact Mickey?'

She stared at Norman.

'Why do you ask that?'

'I just wondered,' he said, innocently. 'If you won't tell him where Jason is, he might think Mickey will.'

'I don't think Mickey would have anything to do with someone like that,' she said. 'He would tell me.'

'Mickey tells you everything?'

'I believe so. My son is not the sort to keep secrets from his mother.'

'That's good,' said Norman.

'Yes, he's a very good boy.'

'Is he into computers and stuff, like my nephew?' asked Norman.

'Well, he spends hours on his computer, but it's all a mystery to me,' she said. 'His teachers seem to think he's good with the technical stuff so I suppose he must be.'

'That's good,' said Norman. 'It's hard to get anywhere these days if you aren't computer literate.'

They passed the rest of the journey with idle chitchat after Norman decided he couldn't ask much more about Mickey without arousing her suspicions.

When they finally got back to her house, he insisted on checking every room in the house and having a look around the garden, even though it was dark.

'Okay, Mia,' he said, eventually. 'I think you're safe enough but make sure you set the burglar alarm just in case.'

'Thank you, you've been very kind. I promise I will do that as soon as you've gone.'

'Well, I guess I'd better get going,' said Norman. He gave her one of his cards. 'If you have any worries or you're not feeling safe, give me a call, and I'll come straight over.'

She studied the card and then looked up at him.

'I'm perturbed about Mickey,' she said. 'I know his father doesn't want me to know where he is, and I don't need to know that, but I haven't heard from Mickey, and he's not answering my calls. I would like to know he's okay. I'm even willing to pay you to find him.'

'Really?' said Norman. 'I thought you didn't want us going near him.'

'I didn't know what you were like before, and you said it was about Lilly Becker.'

'We only want to ask him what she was like. We're not trying to accuse him of anything.'

'Yes, I realise that now,' she said.

'You know, we could find Mickey a lot faster if we had his mobile phone number.'

She seemed to be weighing things up.

'He probably won't answer if you call him.'

'Trust me, we won't call him because it will probably spook him, but we can use the number to locate him. There is one other thing that might help. I don't suppose you have a photograph of your husband we could borrow.'

'One moment,' she said.

18

Slater got to the cafe on the Godden's farm, shortly before it closed.

'Why should I give you Mickey's number?' asked Lewis.

'We need to speak to his father about another matter. If we have Mickey's number, we might be able to track him down, and if he's with his father...'

'How do I know you won't tell his mother where he is?'

'You'd have to trust me.'

'Why should I?'

'Have I given you any reason not to?'

Lewis didn't seem to have an answer to this, so Slater continued speaking.

'The truth is we're not working for Mickey's mother, so we don't have to tell her anything.'

'But you said you were looking for his dad.'

'We're looking for both of them, but we only want to speak to Mickey so we can ask him about Lilly.

'If I gave you his number I'd be betraying his trust.'

Slater nodded.

'I understand that,' he said. 'I think it's good that you feel that way. You're a good friend for Mickey to have.'

'I am?' asked Lewis uncertainly.

'You can relax,' said Slater. 'I'm not going to force you to give me his number. It would save us a lot of time if you did, but if you don't want to, that's okay. You're a man of honour. I admire that.'

'You do?' Lewis blushed. He didn't seem to know what to do with the compliment. He didn't even look sure it was a compliment.

'Can I ask you something else before I go?' asked Slater.

Lewis nodded. 'Okay.'

'You told me Mickey and Lilly weren't boyfriend and girlfriend, but they were like brother and sister.'

'That's right. They used to do stuff together, but they were mates, that's all.'

'Are you sure about that? Only Lilly was a beautiful girl.'

'Yeah, she was,' said Lewis. 'A lot of the guys thought she was hot stuff. She could have taken her pick, but she never did.'

'So why not pick Mickey? Wasn't he interested? I'm sure if I was 14 and I was close to a girl like her I would want to be a bit more than just a friend.'

Lewis smiled, knowingly.

'Yeah, you probably would, but that's because you're interested in girls. Mickey isn't like th—.' But it was too late, Lewis had let the cat out of the bag, and Slater had caught it.

'You mean he's—?'

Quick as a flash, Lewis challenged him.

'You disapprove?' he demanded.

Slater put his hands up in surrender.

'Easy, Lewis, easy,' he said. 'It makes no difference to me either way. I just never gave it a thought. I assumed as Mickey spent so much time with Lilly...'

Lewis's expression changed from aggression to panic.

'You won't tell his mother, will you?'

'Why would I?' asked Slater. 'It's a private matter for you and Mickey to handle as you see fit.'

Lewis was shocked.

'Me? What makes you thi—'

Slater smiled sympathetically. 'As I said, it's none of my business. If your parents love you, they won't care about it one way or the other. Just make sure you choose the right moment to tell them.'

19

It was getting on for 8 pm by the time Norman left Mia Crothers, but he was so pleased with himself he decided to pull over at the first opportunity and call Slater. He was sure Lewis Godden wouldn't have divulged Mickey's phone number, and if he was right this was an opportunity he could not ignore!

'So how did it go with Lewis?' he asked when Slater answered his phone. 'Did he give you Mickey's number?'

'Not exactly,' said Slater.

'What d'you mean not exactly? Either he did, or he didn't.'

'It's complicated.'

Norman couldn't hide his glee.

'He didn't tell you, did he?'

'No,' admitted Slater, wearily.

'"He's a good kid. He'll be happy to help", that's what you said.'

'Yes, thank you for reminding me,' said Slater, testily. 'The thing is Lewis is a loyal friend.'

Norman laughed loudly.

'I have to warn you, smugness is never a good thing,' said Slater.

'That may well be true, but it feels pretty good from here,' said Norman, then more seriously, 'Did Lewis give us anything?'

'Not really. He did tell me that Mickey and Lilly were best friends, but that he and Mickey were a bit more than best friends.'

'Really? That's quite a confession to make to a nosey detective he hardly knows.'

'I don't think he intended to tell me, and at first, he tried to deny it, but then insisted I shouldn't mention it to Mickey's mother. That was enough to convince me it might be worth knowing, although I'm not sure it helps us in any way.'

'So, in reality, you had a wasted journey.'

'You win some, you lose some,' said Slater.

'Unless your name's Norman Norman, and then you win big every time!'

'Ah!' said Slater. 'So you have phoned up to gloat. I thought that's what this must be about. Go on then, what's the big deal?'

'Which one do you want first?'

'Oh God, it sounds like you really have done well.'

'Let's start where you failed,' said Norman, happily. 'I got Mickey's mobile phone number.'

'Jesus, how did you do that?'

'Mia Crothers would like us to find her son and make sure he's okay. I told her it would be a lot easier to find him if we had his mobile number.'

'And she gave it to you?'

'She sure did, and I got a photograph of Jason. At least now we know what the guy looks like.'

'But she hates us. How did you—'

'It's a long story,' said Norman. 'I'll fill you in with the details in the morning. Suffice to say, she no longer hates us, or at least, she might still hate you, but she no longer hates me.'

'What else have you got?'

'Mia Crothers has had two visits from what she describes as a "filthy tramp, who smells disgusting". I only had one thought when she told me.'

'You think it's Tim?'

'It has to be him, doesn't it?'

'But what was he doing there?'

'Yesterday she didn't get to speak to him, but the first time he came to the front door and asked for Jason. He claimed to be an old school friend.'

'Maybe that's the link we were looking for,' said Slater. 'If there's an old family connection it might explain why Mickey created the website.'

'Mia didn't seem to think it was true, and when I asked her if the tramp had asked to see Mickey, she told me there's no way Mickey would have anything to do with a man like that.'

'That's what she thinks. Did you tell her about the website?'

'No, but I did ask her if Mickey was into computers and stuff. She said he spends hours on his laptop and his teachers tell her he's good at that stuff.'

'D'you think we should go and see him again?'

'I thought maybe we could go in the morning unless you have other plans.'

'No, it sounds like a good idea,' said Slater. 'I suppose I ought to congratulate you,' he added, grudgingly, 'but if your head gets too big, you won't be able to get through the office door in the morning.'

'I love it that you can lose with such good grace,' said Norman.

'I had every faith in you, Norm.'

'In that case, breakfast will be on you in the morning.'

Slater laughed. 'Okay, you're on. I'll see you tomorrow.'

He cut the call and put his phone down.

'Sounds like Norm's had a good afternoon,' said Stella.

'Yeah, he's always been good at getting through to the suspects and witnesses I rub up the wrong way. I think his inoffensive charm counters my abrasiveness.'

'You're not abrasive with me.'

'You're not a suspect or a witness,' said Slater, settling back into his seat.

Stella's parents had gone out for the evening, leaving them together on the settee watching football on TV. Slater had never had a girlfriend who enjoyed watching football before, and he was still getting used to the idea of having a partner who shared this particular pleasure.

'I've been doing some digging,' said Stella.

Slater took her hands, looked at the palms then turned them over to stare at the backs, paying particular attention to her nails.

'I would never have guessed. You must have been wearing gloves,' he said, releasing her hands.

Stella's brow creased. 'What?'

'No traces of soil anywhere,' he said. 'Whenever I do any gardening I always find no matter how hard I scrub them afterwards, my fingernails always carry traces of soil. It's a dead giveaway.'

'I wasn't talking about gardening!'

'Well you can't be talking about anything I'm involved in because we agreed you wouldn't poke your nose in—'

Now Stella was sitting up straight, no longer watching the TV.

'Right,' she said, indignantly. 'Let's get something straight. I take exception to your suggestion that I "poke my nose in". I do no such thing.'

Now she had his full attention.

'Hang on a minute,' he said, hastily, turning to face her. 'I didn't mean it like that—'

'And you should understand I didn't agree to stop doing anything,' she spoke over him. 'You made an arbitrary decision which you expected me to accept, but you ignored the fact I have a mind of my own. Big mistake on your part.'

'But it has to stop, Stella.'

'Or what?' she challenged, holding his gaze.

Slater took a moment to think before he spoke. The last thing he wanted was for this to escalate into a big argument. He thought perhaps a different approach might help.

'Okay,' he said. 'Point taken. I'm sorry. You don't poke your nose in. You've actually been very helpful, but you need to understand something. The truth is we're struggling to find enough business to keep us going.'

'Surely that's all the more reason to accept a little help when it's offered.'

'There's more to it than that. We're supposed to be detectives, but we seem to be relying more and more on outside help. It feels as if we're cheating and the fact is we're both finding it a bit uncomfortable. You understand, don't you?'

Stella's expression softened.

'You should have said something before. I was trying to give you a bit of help.'

'I know, and you do help, believe me.'

'Anyway, all I did was hand you some photocopies from an old file. You still have to make sense of it all.'

'Yeah, but it's not just you. There's also Norm's mate Vinnie, up in London. We use him all the time for tech stuff.'

Stella stared at Slater but said nothing. For a moment he thought it would have been better not to have mentioned Vinnie. It was entirely possible he had just given her the opportunity to ask some awkward questions he would rather not have to answer. But instead, she completely wrong-footed him.

'If you're referring to your pet hacker,' she said, her face expressionless, 'I don't think you should tell me anything about him.'

Slater's mouth dropped open.

'He's not a hacker,' he said, automatically.

'Of course, he's a hacker. How else could he access all that information?'

'Ah, yeah, well... but he's a good hacker. He only does it for good causes.'

'Isn't that what they all say?'

'No. I mean, yes. Well, that is... This is one of the reasons we want to stop using him. We're going near the edge, and—'

'Let's face it, Dave, you're not going "near the edge", you're going over it, and by quite a large margin.'

'But what you do is just as bad.'

'There's a limit to what I can get at, and a line I won't cross,' she said, staring intently at him. 'F'r'instance, I wouldn't give you any info relating to a current case. What about your hacker? He can access a lot more than I can. Does he have a line he won't cross?'

Slater stared back at her, but now he was red-faced.

'I'm sorry if knowing about him puts you in a difficult position,' he said.

'At the moment, it doesn't, because I know nothing about him,' she said. 'Which is why I think you shouldn't discuss him with me.'

'This is awkward,' said Slater, sheepishly. 'I'm sorry. Me and my big mouth.'

'You don't have to worry,' she said. 'I'm not going to tell anyone, but I hope your man is as good as you say he is because, sooner or later, he'll make a mistake.'

'He doesn't make mistakes.'

'Come on, Dave. That's a dumb thing to say, and you know it. Everyone makes mistakes, and when he does, if it leads back to you...'

'It won't happen. Honestly, as I said, we're going to stop using him.'

'I think it's for the best,' she said. 'What am I going to do if you end up in prison?'

'I feel the same about you stealing police files,' said Slater. 'What am I going to do if you end up in prison.'

Their faces were just inches apart now, and as they stared into each other's eyes, the inevitable happened and like two magnets, each one unable to resist the other, they were drawn into a long, slow, tender kiss.

Slater settled back on the sofa, his left arm around Stella, snuggled up close beside him. They had missed the last fifteen minutes of the football match, and it was now half time.

'I've been looking into Keeling Security,' she said, quietly, her eyes focused firmly on the TV.

'I take it this means you're losing your job,' he said.

'How do you work that one out?'

'For a start, you're ignoring the fact we use a hacker, and second, you're continuing to take risks that could seriously damage your career. Those two things make me think you're career must already be over, and that's why you don't care.'

'That's where you're wrong,' she said, triumphantly. 'It just so happens I've been asked to look into some old investigations that had been shelved. I have to determine if they're worth re-opening, or if they should be officially closed. The name Keeling Security came up in one of those investigations.'

Now Slater sat up and turned to her.

'Really? In what context?'

'A couple of years ago a complaint was made.'

'What sort of complaint?'

'A householder had been burgled in Norfolk. A couple of days later a rep from Keeling Security turned up suggesting it wouldn't have happened if they had a Keeling security system. The householder thought it was a bit of a coincidence and wanted to know how the salesman could have been aware of the break-in. He suggested it was a scam.'

'Did they say who the salesman was?'

'He was a bit more than just a salesman. He was the Sales Director, Jason Crothers.'

'What happened to the investigation?'

Stella sighed.

'Norfolk asked us to look into Keeling Security, but you know what usually happens to this sort of case when we're short of staff. It was shelved.'

'But someone spoke to Keeling Security, right?'

Stella shook her head.

'Maybe if there had been other complaints, it would have been different, but this was the only one.'

'I can tell you it's not the only one,' said Slater. 'I was trolling the internet this afternoon, looking for Keeling Security, and I found a couple of comments on a website that complained of the same thing.'

'Now that sounds like a pattern,' said Stella, 'but if these people don't complain to us, there's not much we can do.'

'What about if I found that website again and showed those two comments to you? Couldn't you get in touch with those people and see if they wanted to make official complaints?'

'I suppose I could try. Why don't you send me that information in the morning and I'll see what I can do? I won't make any promises though. They won't waste resources on it unless they feel there's a real, solid case to answer.'

'Yeah, I know,' said Slater. 'That's one thing I do remember from my time with the police!'

'Is there anything else you want me to check while I have a legitimate interest in this company?'

Slater thought for a moment.

'Can you get access to their staff list?'

'I'm sure I can think of a reason. Why?'

'See if they have a guy called Josh Ludlow working for them.'

'What d'you want me to do if I find him?'

'I don't think you need to worry about that. I'm quite sure Josh Ludlow doesn't exist. I just want to prove it!'

20

It was close to 10 am on Tuesday when they pulled into the lay-by. As usual, Tim was huddled before his brazier. He turned as they arrived, watched them park, spat on the ground, and then turned back to his fire.

'I don't know if it's just me,' said Slater, as they climbed from the car, 'but I get the impression he doesn't like us.'

'Yeah, he's not exactly subtle about it, is he?'

They strolled across to join Tim, calling a greeting as they approached, but he refused to turn and acknowledge them. Even when they moved around so he couldn't help but see them, he still ignored them.

'You remember we spoke with you about the car that crashed on the road, just there?' Norman waved an arm vaguely in the direction of the road.

'Yeah, I remember,' snapped Tim, jumping to his feet. 'Why does everyone think there's something wrong with my memory?'

Norman raised his hands as if in surrender and took a step back.

'Easy now, Tim,' he said, hastily. 'I didn't mean to imply you had a problem. I just wanted to make sure you recall the conversation we had.'

'I remember, okay?'

'Right,' said Norman. 'Did you know Lilly, the girl who died in the car crash, was just 14 years old? That seems very unfair don't you think? A young life extinguished in a moment.'

Tim looked at Norman as if he were stupid.

'What? You think it's fair when young soldiers get wiped out just for doing their job?'

'No, of course not,' said Norman, 'but at least they know there's a chance that can happen. I don't think Lilly had any idea she might die when she got into that car.'

'If she hadn't stolen the car, she wouldn't have died.'

'What if she didn't steal the car?' asked Norman, patiently.

'Huh? But I thought you said—'

'It was the police who decided she stole the car,' said Slater. 'At the time we assumed they knew what they were talking about, but the more we started to ask questions, the more we began to doubt a kid like her would even think about stealing a car. And then, when you told us you saw someone else at the scene, we began to think maybe she didn't steal it.'

Tim frowned, confused.

'I told you that?'

'A minute ago you said you remembered the conversation,' said Norman. 'Are you now telling me you don't?'

'You're confusing me with all these questions,' said Tim.

'You're the one who claims there's nothing wrong with your memory,' said Slater.

For a moment it looked as if Tim was preparing to launch himself at the detective, but then he seemed to change his mind.

'I only said I thought I saw someone, and when I get stressed I sometimes see things, like I'm back in the war zone.'

'Don't give me that war zone crap,' said Slater. 'You've never been in a bloody war.'

Tim looked as if he was going to argue the point, but instead, he sat down on his upturned bucket and stared into the fire.

'Not going to argue with me?' asked Slater, but Tim ignored the taunt.

'Okay,' said Norman, hastily. 'Let's leave that for now. We can come back to it later.'

Tim stared resolutely into the fire.

'I thought you might like to know I went to see a lady yesterday afternoon,' he said.

'Well, good for you,' said Tim, sulkily.

'I think you know who I mean. Her name is Mia Crothers.'

As Norman spoke Tim was reaching for another log but at the mention of her name he hesitated, then, 'Never heard of her,' he muttered.

'I think you have,' said Norman. 'She lives in a nice, big house, but then you don't need me to tell you that, do you?'

'What's that supposed to mean?'

'You know exactly what it means,' said Norman. 'You were there yesterday afternoon.'

'Bollocks,' said Tim. 'I was here. I never go anywhere. Why would I?'

'Well, that's what I want to know,' said Norman. 'Why did you go there? You frightened the crap out of her when you suddenly appeared at that back window, you know; she was so scared she fell over and banged her head. I had to take her to the hospital.'

Now Tim looked up at Norman, concerned.

'Is she all right?'

'Yes, she is all right. No thanks to you.'

'I just told you, it wasn't me.'

'So why ask if she's all right?'

'It's the decent thing to do, isn't it? It doesn't mean I was there! Anyway, she lives miles away. How would I have got there?'

'You know where she lives, then?' asked Slater.

'I didn't bloody say that!'

'So, how do you know she lives miles away?'

'We're in the middle of nowhere. Everyone lives miles away from here.'

'Don't talk shit. I can see houses from here,' said Slater, pointing back at the village.

'Look, I wasn't there. Like I said, how could I have got there?'

'You've got legs haven't you?' suggested Slater. 'You could've walked there, or maybe someone gave you a lift.'

Tim snorted.

'Oh, yeah, like I've got lots of mates who come over and chauffeur me around.'

'How you got there is irrelevant,' said Norman. 'I know you were there, and you've been there at least one other time.'

'I never bloody was,' said Tim, belligerently.

'Sure you were. That previous time you went to the front door and asked for her husband, Jason. You said you were an old school friend, but Mia told you he wasn't living there, and when you wouldn't leave she shut the door in your face, didn't she?'

'She's making this up,' said Tim. 'I'm telling you I've never been there.'

'Why would she make it up?'

'She's probably one of those people who want me moved on from here.'

'She doesn't even know you live out here,' said Norman, 'and she doesn't live in the village here, so why would she want to move you on?'

'I don't know. When you live rough, you get used to people accusing you of all sorts.'

'Why did you want to see Jason, Tim?' asked Slater. 'What's so important you have to see him?'

'I'm telling you this is all rubbish. You can ask questions until you're blue in the face, but I'm saying nothing.'

'Have you spoken to their son, Mickey?' asked Norman.

Now Tim's eyes narrowed.

'Who?'

'Mickey Crothers. The teenager who built a website for you. Why would he do that if he didn't know you?'

'D'you two talk bollocks all the time, or is it reserved for when you speak to me?'

'Come on, Tim, stop pissing around,' said Slater. 'We know you're lying.'

'Perhaps you were in the Army with Jason Crothers,' suggested Norman. 'Is that where you knew him from?'

'Gawd, bloody hell, how many more questions? For the last time, I have no idea who these people are.'

'You should know we're thinking of reporting you to the police,' said Slater.

'What for? The local coppers know I live here, and they know I'm not doing anyone any harm.'

'But do they know you're not a war hero like you claim to be?' asked Slater.

'What are you talking about? I did my time. I was in Afghanistan. I got blown up.'

'Now who's talking bollocks?' asked Slater. 'These things can be checked you know. That's how we know you're a fraud. You've never been in the Army, have you?'

Tim licked his lips and glared at the two detectives.

'I've got nothing to say. Now piss off and leave me alone!'

Slater shook his head.

'Sorry Tim, we can't do that.'

'Well, if you've got time to waste, that's up to you, but I'm saying nothing!'

'It's a pity you're not listening,' said Norman. 'We're trying to help you, Tim.'

'Maybe he's not listening because we're using the wrong name,' said Slater. 'Perhaps he'll talk if we call him Harvey.'

It was as if time had stood still for a few seconds, and then Tim jumped to his feet, fists raised.

'I don't know what your game is,' he roared, 'but I've had enough.'

He took a couple of steps towards Slater who stood his ground and smiled.

'Now, if you were a real war hero, I might be worried,' he said, 'but

I know you're not. You're just a guy who's been living rough for years, and I reckon that means I don't have much to worry about.'

This wasn't quite the reaction Tim had been hoping for, and he took a step back.

'That's not a good idea, Tim,' said Norman. 'Ole Dave there might look soft and flabby, but I bet he could put you on the deck with one hand tied behind his back. Let's face it, you're not exactly at the peak of physical fitness, are you?'

Tim glared at Slater, but took another step back and lowered his hands.

'That's better,' said Norman. 'Sit back down there in front of your fire and calm down. We haven't come here to fight with you, and we're not going to report you to the police. We want to talk because we think you might know things that could help us find out what happened to the girl in the crash.'

'I thought you were looking for a missing boy?'

'Yeah, we are,' said Norman, 'but the two are linked so anything you know might help.'

Tim thought about it for a minute or two, then slowly settled back on his bucket.

'What d'you want to know?'

'Let's start with Jason Crothers. Why did you go to his house?'

'I want to kill him.'

There was stunned silence, and then Norman broke the silence.

'Don't you think that's a bit extreme?' he asked.

'That man is the devil incarnate. It's going to take something extreme to stop him.'

'Yeah, but murder?' said Slater. 'You'd be in prison for the rest of your life! You don't want that.'

'An eye for an eye, that's what I want,' said Tim. 'Anyway, what am I going to miss if I'm in prison?' He looked at his surroundings. 'I'd have a roof over my head, washing facilities, proper meals. I'd be much better off, wouldn't I?'

'So, what's the story?' asked Norman. 'We figure the Afghanistan thing is bullshit, right?'

Tim sighed.

'As you discovered, I was never in the Army, but people are more tolerant when you have a story like that. No-one wants to listen to a sob story like mine, but mention PTSD and the Army, and it's a whole new world.'

'You know it's wrong, don't you?' asked Norman.

'Yeah, of course, I know, but I don't tell anyone unless they ask, and I don't ask anyone for money.'

Slater thought about the website and was tempted to argue the point about not asking for money, but decided it would only sour the atmosphere. They could argue about the rights and wrongs another time. Right now it would be better to encourage Tim to talk.

'But you haven't always lived in a car, have you?' he said. 'No-one does that by choice, so there must be a good reason.'

Tim looked thoughtfully from Norman to Slater, then he seemed to come to a decision and pointed to two buckets alongside the car.

'Take a seat, and I'll tell you.'

They took a bucket each and sat either side of Tim, who was now staring intently into the fire.

'You're right, I haven't always been like this,' he began. 'I used to have a good job, a nice house in Harrogate, a lovely wife, and a beautiful daughter. Light of my life she was, my little Jeanie.' A sad little smile passed across his face at the memory of his daughter.

'So what happened?' asked Norman.

'Jason Crothers is what happened. He's a womaniser who likes to destroy families. Don't get me wrong, I understand it takes two to tango, and she had a choice, but when he gets a woman in his sights, he's relentless. It took him a long time, but eventually, he convinced my wife she'd have a better life with him, so she took Jeanie and left me. Then, within a week he just walked away and left them both.'

'Jeez, I'm sorry,' said Norman. 'I know what it's like when your wife does something like that. It's hard to deal with.'

'I might have coped with her leaving me, we might even have got back together in time, but it got worse than that.' He seemed to be choking on the words, and for a moment he stopped speaking and stared at the fire.

'It's okay,' said Norman. 'You don't have to say any mo—.'

'Jeanie was just fourteen years old. She had her whole life in front of her but, because of that man and what he did, she committed suicide!'

There was a sudden almost eerie silence.

'Oh, Jesus!' was all Slater could say.

'When you say "because of what he did", d'you mean because he broke up your family?' asked Norman, tentatively.

Tim tore his gaze from the fire and turned to look at Norman.

'That's what I thought at first. I used to be in the security business, too, you see. I had my own company. We were small, but we were rivals to Keeling Security. So, it made sense to think Crothers had done it to get at me. Destroy my family, destroy me, destroy my business.'

'Oh, my,' said Norman. 'I'm sorry. We had no idea—'

'My wife blamed herself,' continued Tim. 'And before I knew it she, too, had taken an overdose. They were both gone because of that man, and he walked away without a care in the world.'

No-one spoke for a couple of minutes. But then no-one knew what to say.

'I couldn't cope with that,' said Tim, finally. 'I kept thinking if I'd only been living with my wife at the time I could have stopped her taking those pills. But now they were both gone, and it was all I could think about. Nothing else mattered, but I found if I got drunk enough I could stop thinking, just for a while. I lost what really made my life worthwhile, but you'd be surprised how quickly you can drink the rest of your life away, too. The thing is I didn't care. As long as I was pissed, I could forget for a while.'

'How long have you been sober?' asked Slater.

'Just over four years now.'

'That's quite an achievement, after what happened,' said Norman. 'How did you manage to do it?'

'It's amazing what you can do when you discover a purpose.'

'So what is your purpose?'

'A vicar scraped me off the floor one night and took me to a hostel. He spent a week keeping me clean, listening to me. He convinced me it wasn't my fault, and that blaming myself wasn't going to change things. He helped me find a new focus.'

'Did he know your new focus was finding Jason Crothers?' asked Slater.

A wry smile crossed Tim's face. 'I didn't think it would be fair to share that with him. Making him feel guilty wouldn't help would it?'

'Did you go to see Mia Crothers with the intention of hurting her?' asked Norman.

Tim looked appalled at the idea.

'No, I did not! Why would I do that?'

'An eye for an eye, isn't that what you said?'

'Yeah, but not literally. I want Jason Crothers to pay with his life, not the rest of them. They haven't done anything to me, have they? I just wanted her to tell me where he lives.'

'This revenge idea is insane,' said Norman.

'Yeah, well maybe I am insane. God knows I have enough reason to be, don't I?'

'We can't just stand by and let you kill someone, no matter what he's done.'

'I can't kill him until I find him, and right now I have no idea where he is.'

'You need to stop looking,' warned Norman. 'Even we haven't found him yet, and we have more resources than you.'

He gave Norman a knowing smile.

'Well, in that case, you'd better hope you find him before I do.'

21

'I haven't always lived with my parents, you know,' said Stella.

Slater was surprised by this sudden change in the conversation, but he did his best not to show it.

'I kinda guessed that,' he said.

She gave him an enquiring look.

'You did tell me you once had a husband who was an arse, remember?' he said, defensively.

'You're right, I did,' she recalled, 'and yet you've never asked me about him.'

He shrugged. 'It's really none of my business, is it? Besides, I figure you'll tell me about him if you want me to know.'

'The thing is, I divorced him a couple of years before the attack.'

'Right,' he said. For moment Slater couldn't see where this was going, but only for a moment.

'Jesus. You don't mean he was the one who—'

'What, attacked me? Good God, no. What I meant was—'

'—after your divorce, you had a place of your own, but after the attack, you didn't want to be there on your own,' finished Slater.

She nodded, her eyes downcast.

'That's about the size of it,' she said, sadly. Then much brighter, 'You should be a detective with your deductive powers.'

He smiled. 'Yeah, so I've been told. I've heard there's not much money in it though.'

They had a quiet chuckle at his joke, then he spoke again. 'So, what did you do with this place, sell it?'

'Oh, no. My dad wouldn't let me. He said selling it would be like admitting defeat.'

'And was he right?'

She smiled, fondly.

'I didn't think he was at the time, but my dad is one of those annoying people who usually turn out to be right about everything.'

'So he was right.'

'He says wisdom comes with age.'

'The more I hear about your dad, the more I like him,' said Slater.

'He likes you,' she said.

'Ah, yes,' he said, 'but he hardly knows me, does he?'

'He thinks you're very patient.'

'Well, there you go, that proves my point. People who have known me for a while wouldn't agree.'

'Well I agree with him,' she said. 'I think you've been incredibly patient. It can't be easy trying to date someone who needs to keep you at arm's length.'

'It's not that bad,' he said. 'Besides you're much more confident with me than you were in the beginning.'

'A lot of men wouldn't—'

'And that's their loss, isn't it?' He winked at her. 'Anyway, maybe I think it'll be worth the wait.'

His face had turned scarlet, and he winced inside as soon as the words left his mouth. How crass was that? What on earth was he thinking? He was almost too embarrassed to look at her, but to his great surprise, she was laughing.

'It's all right,' she giggled. 'You don't have to look so horrified.'

'I'm sorry,' he said. 'I didn't mean—'

'Now listen,' she said, sternly. 'I'm never going to move on if you're going to treat me like I'm made of glass.'

'Yes, but—'

She raised a hand to silence him.

'Stop speaking, and listen to me,' she said. 'I feel I've spent the last couple of years living behind a wall, protected at home by my dad, protected at work by being stuck behind a desk, and now being protected by you. But now that's all got to change. I'm at a crossroads in my life, and it's time to move on, so I'm making some choices.'

Slater was impressed. She sounded more positive than he had ever seen her. He wanted to hear more, but he didn't want to spoil the moment, so he kept quiet.

'It's a big step, but the first thing I've decided is that I can't expect you to wait around for me forever.'

This wasn't what Slater wanted to hear. 'Hang on,' he said. 'You can't dump me. I'm not in any hurry. I'll wait as long as—'

She reached across the table for his hand, her eyes shining.

'I'm not dumping you, stupid,' she said.

He looked confused. 'But you just said—'

'I want us to be like a normal couple. I'm not saying it's going to be easy, but if we take one step at a time... What do you say? Will you help me move on?'

'Jesus, Stella. That's a stupid question. I'd do anything to help you, you should know that.'

'Of course, I know it,' she said, 'but I wanted to hear you say it. I don't want to take anything for granted.'

A waiter appeared with their food. They sat back and waited until he had gone.

'What else have you decided?' asked Slater.

'As I said, I have a small flat. It's not far from mum and dad. It's been empty all this time, but mum and I go round once or twice a week to collect my post and keep it tidy. I want to start living there again.'

'Wow. That's another big step,' he said.

'This is the biggest,' she said. 'I was thinking maybe starting with just one or two nights a week.'

'Small steps. Yeah. It sounds like a good idea,' he said, encouragingly.

'I'm told every journey is a collection of steps, but it can't start until you take the first one,' she said.

Slater beamed at her. 'Straight out of the Norman Norman guide to positive thinking, that one.'

'The thing is, I'm not sure I can make that first step without some help,' she said.

'Okay. I said I'll help. What do you want me to do?'

She stared intently into his eyes. 'I was wondering if you'd come and stay with me.'

'Bloody hell,' said Slater. He couldn't think of anything else to say.

'Don't you want to?'

'It's not that,' he said. 'It just seems a huge step from not touching you to sleeping with you.'

'Ah, yes,' she said, awkwardly. 'That wasn't quite what I meant.'

'Oh, I see, I think.'

'I'm not saying I don't want to,' she said. 'But I can't promise—'

'It's okay,' he said. 'I can sleep on the settee.'

'It's not very comfortable.'

'I'll manage. It's only going to be for one night at a time.'

'I'm sorry—'

'Don't apologise, Stella. I'm really proud of you, and I'd love to be there to support you even if it means sleeping on the floor.'

'You see. I said you were very patient.'

He smiled at her.

'You'll have to show me where this flat is.'

'I was planning to after we leave here.'

Slater couldn't hide his surprise. 'Oh! Right.'

'Is that okay?'

'Sure.'

'Well, come on then,' she said, pushing her chair back. 'We can pay on the way out.'

. . .

'I NEARLY FORGOT, there's something else I meant to tell you,' she said, once they were in his car.

'Is it going to be another surprise?'

'I'm pretty sure it will be.'

'I'm not sure I can handle any more of your surprises tonight.'

'Oh, it's not about me. It's to do with your case.'

Slater sighed.

'Yes, I know,' she said, 'but you'll thank me for this.'

He glanced quickly across at her.

'What is it, then?' he said, slowing to turn right.

'I managed to find the post mortem report for Lilly Becker. Did her mother tell you she was sexually active?'

Slater nearly missed his turning.

'But she was only fourteen!'

She looked at him sympathetically.

'Which planet have you been living on?' she said. 'Do you really think they all wait until they're legal?'

'Of course, I don't, but her mother never mentioned anything about that.'

'I don't think it was ever made public.'

'What does that mean?'

'I got the feeling it wasn't considered relevant to the investigation at the time, so it was hushed up to spare the family any embarrassment.'

'Not relevant?'

'It didn't make her crash the car, did it? She was on her own.'

'So they say,' said Slater.

'All the evidence—'

'Yeah, I know about all the evidence.'

'But you don't agree?'

'Let's just say I have my doubts.'

'Are you going to share?'

He cast a quick smile in her direction.

'And have you involved even more? No, I don't think so.'

She pouted. 'You can be such a meanie sometimes.'

'Yeah, I know, and I'm afraid this is definitely one of those times. Now, where's this flat of yours.'

She pointed ahead. 'Take the next left and follow the road round to the right.'

22

'My, my,' said Norman when Slater walked into the office on Wednesday morning. 'Do you look like the cat that got the cream, or what?'

Slater tried his hardest not to blush, but there was just enough of a hint to prove Norman right.

'Aha! There it is, the glowing face that tells us Norm's right again. C'mon then spill the beans, or is it too embarrassing to tell?'

Slater cursed under his breath and wondered how come he was so easy for Norman to read? His face had given him away, yet again, but now what was he going to say? Norm was his best friend, but even so, there was no way he was going to share what had happened last night.

'It's okay,' said Norman. 'You don't have to tell me. I slept at yours last night, so I know you didn't come home.'

'Actually, you're wrong,' said Slater. 'That's not why I'm looking pleased with myself.'

'Oh, really?'

'Remember the other night when you phoned me to crow about what you'd found out that I hadn't?'

'You mean Mickey's mobile number?'

'That's right.'

'You got something even better?'

'I don't know if it's actually better, but it certainly adds a new dimension to this case.'

'Come on then, let's hear it.'

'Stella got a peek at the PM report into Lilly Becker's death. It turns out Lilly was sexually active.'

'Is that it?' asked Norman.

Slater was crestfallen.

'What d'you mean "is that it?" Isn't that enough?'

'You think she's the only fourteen-year-old who lost her virginity?'

'Of course not, but—'

'She's been Mickey's girlfriend since they were tots. She was a pretty girl, and he's a good looking boy. What d'you expect?'

'You forget what Lewis told me about him and Mickey.'

'That might be how Mickey and Lewis are now, but what about two years ago?'

'I'm pretty sure he meant Mickey had never seen Lilly that way, and that they were always just mates.'

'I take it she wasn't carrying anyone's DNA inside her that day?'

'That would have been interesting, wouldn't it?' said Slater. 'In a way, it's a pity. If there had been traces of foreign DNA, maybe they wouldn't have been so quick to close the investigation.'

'How come this was kept quiet?'

'It wasn't considered relevant as Lilly was found on her own, so it was kept quiet to save embarrassment to Lilly's family. That's what I meant when I said it was a pity there was no foreign DNA.'

'Well, I'll admit it's intriguing, but in itself, it doesn't prove anything.'

'What if she was in a relationship with someone, and he was driving the car? Suppose the plan was to go for a drive, and then have sex when they got back?'

'That's pure speculation,' said Norman.

'Well, yeah, maybe, but it fits the scenario,' argued Slater.

'Only if you have a boyfriend and you can place him at the scene, and even then you couldn't prove they intended to have sex afterwards.'

'I'm beginning to wonder whose side you're on,' said Slater, sulkily.

'Look, I know you like to think outside the box, and you've been right on the money on more than one occasion, but sometimes you get carried away, and then you don't see the wood for the trees.'

'I just think this wasn't as open and shut as—'

'I understand where you're coming from,' said Norman. 'But without any evidence, it's just guesswork. I certainly don't want to put any wild theories into Lizzie Becker's head unless we can back them up with some hard evidence.'

'Speaking of Lizzie Becker,' said Slater. 'Don't you think we ought to ask her about Lilly? I mean, she never mentioned it when she came to see us.'

'I can understand that. If she was told it wasn't relevant, why tell us?'

'Yes, I understand it, too, but what if she knew about it, and knows who Lilly was seeing? That could have a huge bearing on who sent that message, and what happened the night Lilly died. Maybe then my speculation won't seem quite so wild.'

'It'll be an awkward conversation.'

'Yes, I know, but we ought to update her anyway. We can always say we came across some information and we need her to confirm it.'

There was a loud "ping" from Norman's laptop. He sat down and clicked into his email.

'I HAVE AN EMAIL FROM VINNIE,' said Norman. 'He says he's managed to track the location of the PAYG mobile phone when the text was sent to Lizzie Becker.'

'Jesus, that guy really can do anything,' said Slater, with grudging admiration. 'So, where was it?'

'East Winton.'

'Not in the lay-by again?'

'No, it was in the village.'

'Does he know where?'

'It wasn't on long enough for him to get an exact location, but it's definitely in East Winton somewhere.'

'Right. So, it could have been a local dog walker who switched on the phone on Friday, and it could be the same person today.'

'Yeah, maybe,' said Norman.

'What's up?' asked Slater. 'You don't look very happy.'

Norman frowned.

'Vinnie says he's also identified the actual phone it was sent from.'

'Can he do that, as well as find it?'

'It looks that way. He says that although it's a PAYG sim card, it's the actual mobile phone that belonged to Lilly Becker.'

'What?'

'That's what he says,' said Norman. 'I think it's got something to do with each phone having a unique ID number of some sort, although I'm not sure if that's exactly how it works. There again I don't need to know how. I trust Vinnie, he's never been wrong before.'

'This could explain why they never found Lilly's phone,' said Slater. 'Either someone else had it all along, or it was lost, and someone found it.'

'And I guess Lilly's old account was closed so that the sim card wouldn't have worked,' added Norman. 'Hence the need for a PAYG sim card.'

'I suppose it's possible it could have been lost in the accident,' said Slater, 'but I can't believe it could have been lying there, exposed to the weather for all this time, and still work.'

'So, what are you saying? You think someone stole it from Lilly before the accident?'

'It could be that, or maybe someone came across the accident before the police arrived on the scene.'

'But I thought there was no evidence to suggest anyone else was involved.'

'Yeah, I know, but what if the phone was thrown from the car making it easy to pick up without leaving any trace?'

Norman didn't look convinced.

'Of course,' added Slater, 'there is a third possibility.'

'What's that?' asked Norman.

'What if Lilly wasn't alone?'

'That again? I thought the lack of any evidence meant that idea had been ruled out by the police.'

'What if they got it wrong?'

'But, if there was no evidence—'

'Just hear me out a minute,' insisted Slater. 'I took Stella down to the motor museum near Southampton yesterday. They have several Austin Healeys down there. After a lot of persuasion, Stella was allowed to sit in one while I took photos of her. Of course, what she was really doing was trying to see if she could reach the pedals.'

'I thought you didn't want her involved.'

'I didn't, but can you think of a better way of finding this out? Stella's at least six inches taller than Lilly, and she could barely touch the pedals if she perched right on the edge of the driver's seat. There's no way Lilly could have been driving that car unless she had enormous blocks strapped to her feet!'

Norman silently absorbed what Slater had said.

'Let me get this straight,' he said, finally. 'You're saying you think someone else was in the car, survived the crash, and then ran off and left Lilly to die without leaving the slightest trace?'

'Why not?'

'You think one person gets killed by the crash and the other escapes unscathed? Are you serious?'

Now it was Slater's turn to stop and think.

'I suppose you have a point,' he conceded. 'But Lilly wasn't wearing a seat belt, so it's not impossible, and it does explain how the car got there if Lilly couldn't reach the pedals to drive it.'

'But Lilly was found in the driver's seat.'

'Or was she?' argued Slater. 'The way I read it, the car was upside down, and she was found on the driver's side. That's not necessarily the same thing, is it? With no seatbelt on, she could have been thrown from the passenger side.'

Norman sighed. He studied Slater's face for a few moments before he delivered his opinion of Slater's theory.

'If you don't mind me saying, you seem to have become obsessed with the idea Lilly didn't steal that car, and now you're trying to make the evidence fit your scenario instead of accepting it at face value.'

Norman's dismissive attitude irritated Slater, but he couldn't decide if his partner genuinely thought it was a crazy idea, or he was playing devil's advocate. In the end, he decided now wasn't the time to argue. It could wait until he found some more compelling evidence to back up his theory.

'Okay. Maybe you're right, and I've got it all wrong about there being another driver,' he conceded, grudgingly. 'In which case, I go back to my other theory that someone came upon the scene, saw the phone, and took it.'

'I think that's a more likely scenario,' agreed Norman. 'But d'you seriously think someone took the phone and didn't do anything about helping Lilly?'

'I don't know, Norm. Maybe she was already dead, and they couldn't help her, but they saw the phone and took it anyway. Perhaps they didn't even look to see if Lilly was still alive. Let's face it, there are plenty of unscrupulous people around.'

Norman pulled a face that acknowledged the fact, no matter how distasteful.

'Okay, maybe you're right about that, so why wait until now to activate the phone?'

'I haven't got that far, Norm. It's your mate who says it's Lilly's phone. I'm just speculating as to what might have happened to it since the crash.'

'I guess that's all the more reason to go back and speak to Tim,' said Norman.

'But what use would a mobile phone be to someone like him? I mean, who's he going to call? And how would he charge it? He can't exactly plug it into his car while he's driving around, can he?'

'Maybe he doesn't have the phone, but he saw someone near the crash, remember? Maybe he saw a bit more than he was letting on.'

23

'Hi Tim,' said Norman.

'Jesus! Not you two again. D'you know why I live out here in an old car, in this unused lay-by?' He didn't wait for a reply. 'It's because no-one else ever comes here bothering me. At least they didn't until you two found me.'

Norman smiled.

'Yeah, sorry about that,' he said. 'Trust me, I'd rather not have to keep coming back, but you see we have a friend up in London who suggested we should come back.'

'Friend? What friend? I'm surprised you two have any friends.'

'To tell the truth, he's not really a friend of mine,' said Slater. He nodded at Norman. 'He's Norm's mate. To be honest I find him arrogant, and annoying, but even so, I know he's one of the cleverest buggers I've ever met, and he's never been wrong yet.'

'Wrong about what?'

'He's what you might call a geek,' explained Slater. 'He's shit hot when it comes to anything technical like computers, or mobile phones.'

'Yeah, so?'

'He's so clever if a mobile phone is switched on, and we give him the number, he can tell us where it's located. Now, why don't you take a guess why he suggested we should come back here?'

Tim seemed to be having difficulty swallowing.

'I don't know what you're talking about,' he mumbled.

'So you don't have a mobile phone?'

'What good would a mobile phone be to me? Anyway, I can't afford a mobile phone.'

'Yeah, we get that you couldn't buy one, but you didn't have to, did you? The mobile phone you have is the one that belonged to Lilly Becker.'

Tim stared at the ground.

'What happened?' asked Slater, bitterly. 'Did you go over to the car, see she was dying, and help yourself to her phone? She was just a kid for God's sake! Did you leave her there to die on her own?'

Tim slumped back against the car and slid down until he sat on his haunches. A few stray tears rolled down his cheeks.

'D'you really think I could do that after losing my own fourteen-year-old daughter?'

Slater hadn't thought about that, and now he felt like a complete arse.

'So, what did happen?'

'It wasn't anything like you seem to think,' said Tim. 'I already told you what happened. There was someone there. I saw him lifting her from the car. I thought he was helping her, so I ran and hid.'

Slater looked round at Norman who placed a warning hand on his arm and then crouched down in front of Tim.

'I've been doing this for a long time, Tim,' he said, quietly. 'And when you do something for long enough, you develop instincts, like gut feelings, you know?'

Tim nodded.

'Now, my gut says you're not telling the truth,' continued Norman. 'What do you say?'

'I dunno. What d'you want me to say?'

'Don't get clever now, Tim. We're talking about a young girl, just like your daughter, who died in what we think are suspicious circumstances. I believe you know a whole lot more than you're saying. I would even suggest you didn't run and hide.' He indicated the bank between the lay-by and the road. 'I think you were up at the top of that bank, where you couldn't be seen, so why would you need to hide? I think it's much more likely you stayed to watch the whole thing, maybe even until the police arrived.'

'I didn't see all of it.'

'Okay, but you definitely saw a man, right?' asked Norman.

Tim nodded.

'Yeah, I can recall it quite clearly,' he said.

'And when we spoke before you told us you thought he was lifting Lilly from the car, right?'

'Yeah, that's right.'

'Was he trying to get her away from the car? Maybe he thought it was going to burst into flames and he was trying to save her.'

'He was trying to move her, but I don't think he was trying to save her.'

Slater felt his scalp tingling.

'Can you describe him?' he asked.

Tim shook his head.

'It was too dark to see most of the time, but every now and then the moon came out from behind the clouds, and I got a glimpse. That's how I could make out what he was doing, but I never got to see his face.'

'Can you remember which side of the car he was on?'

'He was on this side,' said Tim, with certainty.

'Are you sure?'

'I wouldn't have been able to see him if he had been the other side, would I?'

'You gave us a really vague description last time,' said Norman. 'If you were watching him for a few minutes you must have got an impression of how big he was, and how he moved. Did he look like an old guy or a young guy?'

'Young.'

'How tall?'

'Can't say for sure. Not a big guy. Probably five six to five nine.'

Slater was trying to recall the drawings and photographs he had seen of the crash scene. The car had been heading into East Winton which meant the driver would have been on the side nearest the lay-by. But then the car had overturned when the driver lost control. That would put the driver on the far side. So, if Lilly was driving, why was the man lifting her from this side?

'Norm,' he said, quietly.

Norman looked over his shoulder.

'Can I have a word?'

Norman turned back to Tim. 'Are you okay?' he asked.

Tim nodded.

'I'm going to give you a few minutes,' said Norman, getting to his feet. 'I'm just going to speak with my partner, okay?'

Tim nodded and then buried his head in his knees.

'Jeez, he's in a right state,' he said quietly to Slater as they took a few steps away. 'Did you have to mention his daughter?'

'I didn't mean to upset him like that,' said Slater. 'But for a minute there I thought he was saying he'd left Lilly to—'

'Yeah, I get it,' said Norman, a little testily.

'He's talking, isn't he?'

'Yes, but maybe next time you could try to be a little more thoughtful.'

'Okay. I admit I was in the wrong, but I've said I'm sorry.'

'Maybe you're saying sorry to the wrong guy,' said Norman.

'Look, I get the point. I'll apologise in a minute.'

'So what did you want to speak about?'

'He just said he saw a man lifting Lilly from the car, right? That's twice now. You must be convinced now.'

'Yeah, he did say it, but you can see the state of him. I wouldn't get too excited about it.'

'What? You're not going to tell me he's making it up, are you?'

'No, I'm just saying the details might not be absolutely correct. I mean last time he couldn't even say for sure if it was a man or a woman, now he's saying a young guy below average height.'

'Okay. But, for the minute, let's assume he's telling the truth.'

Norman sighed.

'We've been here before,' he said. 'But okay, go on, I'll buy it.'

'He said the guy was on this side of the car.'

'Yeah, and?'

'The car was heading out of the village, and had turned over.'

'So, maybe he couldn't get to her from the other side.'

'But the photos show the driver's door was torn off in the crash.'

Norman opened his mouth to speak, but then stopped and stared at Slater.

'If Lilly were driving, she would have been on the other side,' continued Slater.

'But she was found on the driver's side,' said Norman.

'Yes,' countered Slater, 'but if what we just heard is true, that could be because someone put her there.'

'Her fingerprints were all over the steering wheel, and the gear stick.'

'C'mon, Norm. She was dead. I think the guy dragged her over to the driver's side, placed her hands all over the steering wheel and gear stick, and then fled the scene.'

Norman looked sceptical. 'How come there were no other prints anywhere?'

'There were other prints, but they belonged to members of the Crothers family.'

'Yeah, well, that's no surprise; it was their car,' said Norman.

'Or, maybe it's no surprise because one of them was driving that night,' suggested Slater.

'You seem to forget they all have alibis that prove they can't have been there.'

'Okay, so maybe the driver was wearing gloves. Perhaps whoever it was knew about forensics and keeping things clean.'

Norman still wasn't convinced. 'Yeah, I suppose that's possible.' He cast a glance at Tim. 'You know this isn't exactly what we came here to ask him about. We were supposed to be asking about the phone.'

'Yeah, I know, but you can't continue ignoring what he said about someone being at the crash scene.'

'Okay, I get the point,' said Norman. 'But don't lean on him about that any more. We still have to find out about the phone, and I don't want to push him over the edge.'

'D'you think I should call Kelly Sellars?'

'That might be a good idea,' said Norman, 'although I expect he'll go apeshit when he sees how upset Tim is.'

'Let me go and apologise first. Maybe he'll get himself together before Kelly gets here.'

As Norman had predicted Kelly Sellars was not impressed when he arrived. He spent a few minutes seeing to Tim and then began berating the two detectives.

'You really ought to be ashamed of yourselves. The poor guy put his life on the line for people like you, and all y—'

'Don't talk bollocks!' snapped Slater.

'I beg your pardon?'

'He's no more a bloody war hero than I am.'

'Of course, he is. How d'y—'

'D'you think we're pig-shit stupid?' asked Norman.

'I'm sorry?'

'We're not a pair of DIY detectives, doing this for a laugh. We have over forty years of experience between us. Don't you realise there are ways of checking out who people are, and what their real stories are?'

Sellars' face had turned cherry red, and his self-righteousness seemed to fade before their very eyes.

'Er, well, I er...'

'Tim's real name is Harvey Sellars,' said Slater.

'Quite a coincidence, you both having the same surname,' said Norman. 'But then maybe not so much, seeing as he's your older brother.'

'And he's never been in the Army, as you well know,' added Slater.

'Ah. Right. I see.'

'Didn't he tell you we were here yesterday?' asked Norman.

'Yesterday?'

'He didn't tell you?' asked Slater. 'And you think we're amateurs? How the hell do you expect to keep a lie going if you two don't keep each other informed?'

'So, he told you the whole story?' asked Sellars.

'If you mean about his wife, and daughter, and how he's looking for Jason Crothers, then yes, he told us. Is there anything else we should know?'

'I wouldn't be the one to ask. We may be brothers, but he's never really confided in me. To be honest, you probably know as much as me.'

'Who's idea was it to come up with the war hero story?' asked Slater.

'That's all his idea. He seems to think it's okay to lie if it hides an uncomfortable truth.'

'You know it's against the law to impersonate a member of the Services?'

'I've told him, but he won't listen. He says it won't be for much longer, and then he'll move on and stop using that story.'

'Move on?'

'I assume he means when he's found out where he can find Jason Crothers.'

'D'you think he'll really kill him?'

Sellars pulled a face.

'I don't know. Like I said we're not really close. Sometimes I think I don't know him at all.'

'Yet you still look out for him.'

Sellars shrugged.

'At the end of the day he's still my brother, and he needs help.'

'In case you didn't realise it, helping him to find someone so he can murder them is a crime called conspiracy to murder. You'll end up in prison too.'

'I'm not going to turn my back on him, am I?'

'So you're happy to help him kill someone, and yet you let him live out here in an old car? Those two things seem to be at odds,' said Norman.

'The only help he gets from me is food and water. It's his choice, to live out here. I've offered him a room with me, but he's not interested.'

'I assume you know he's been to the Crothers' house,' said Norman.

Sellars nodded. 'Yes, I know about that.'

'So you're okay with him hassling Mia Crothers?'

'All he wants from her is Jason's address.'

'Did you know he went there yesterday?'

'Of course, he does, Norm,' said Slater. Then, addressing Sellars, 'You drove him there, waited while he went up to the house, and then drove him back, didn't you?'

Sellars' eyes widened.

'So that's why I didn't see him when I was over there,' said Norman. 'Is he going to murder her, too?'

'Of course not.'

'So, you'd be surprised if I said I had to take her to A&E yesterday after you two had been there?'

'What? No. She fell over. He told me. He wouldn't lay a finger on her. I told you, he just wants that address.'

'She doesn't have it.'

'Yes, I think Tim realises that now. I don't think he'll bother her again.'

'What about the son, Mickey?'

'We didn't know who he was at first. He started coming here a few weeks after the accident. He just used to sit and stare at the road. Tim got talking to him one day, and they ended up becoming friends.'

'Mickey comes here?' asked Norman.

'Yes. I thought you knew.'

'We know now,' muttered Slater.

'What I meant was, is Mickey in any danger?' asked Norman.

'Good Lord, no. Tim likes him. He wouldn't hurt him.'

'You are aware Mickey's girlfriend was the one who died in the accident?' asked Norman.

'Yes, I believe that's why he started coming here.'

'Do you know if he ever said anything about the accident?'

'I don't think so. He told me he wasn't there. What could he know?'

'What about you, Mr Sellars? Do you know anything?'

'I only know what I read in the newspapers.'

'The police never found the mobile phone of the girl who died,' said Slater. 'You wouldn't know anything about that?'

The three had been standing in a vague circle as they spoke, but now Sellars took a step back and folded his arms.

'Me? Why would I know anything about that?'

'I just wondered if Tim had ever mentioned it.'

'Why would he? That was over two years ago, wasn't it? I expect she lost it somewhere, or maybe someone stole it, before the accident.'

'That's what the police suggested,' said Norman. 'The thing is every mobile phone has its own unique identification number. You would have thought if someone had stolen it they would have put a new SIM card in and used it, or perhaps sold it to someone else so they could use it. Yet that phone has never been identified in use. Or at least it hadn't been until a few days ago.'

Sellars licked his lips but said nothing.

'We had a trace on that particular mobile phone,' said Slater. 'When it was switched on for the first time since the accident, guess where it was?'

Sellars licked his lips again.

'Not going to take a guess?' asked Slater. 'Okay, I'll tell you. It was first identified in this very location, more or less right where we're standing now.'

'I wouldn't know anything about that.'

'The next time it was identified in the village just over there,' Slater pointed towards the village. 'You live in that village, don't you, Mr Sellars?'

Sellars swallowed hard.

'What are you suggesting?'

'I'm sure it's just a coincidence,' said Slater. 'Don't you agree, Norm?'

'Yeah,' said Norman. 'I'm sure that's all it is. I can't see someone like Mr Sellars, sending a malicious text message to the dead girl's mother, can you?'

Sellars swallowed again.

'Malicious text message?'

'Oh, didn't I say,' said Norman. 'The reason we got involved in this is that someone sent a text to the dead girl's mother, from the dead girl's phone.'

'That would be bad enough,' added Slater, 'but the text was made to look like it was sent by the dead girl. You can imagine how upset her mother was.'

Sellars glanced at Tim.

'We never sent any text me—'

Sellars stopped speaking, but it was too late.

'Oh, please, don't stop,' said Slater. 'You've already given the game away, so you might as well spit the rest of it out.'

'I'm guessing "we" is you and Tim, right?' suggested Norman. 'Of course, we could call the police, and let the two of you explain it to them.'

'What's it going to be, Kelly?' asked Slater. 'Tell us now, or you both get arrested and interviewed under caution.'

'You could end up with criminal records,' added Norman.

Sellars sighed. He was trapped, and he knew it.

'We'd better go and join Tim,' he said. 'He needs to know about this.'

As they walked the few yards back, Sellars called out to Tim.

'Tim, they know about the phone.'

When he looked up Tim's face was as black as thunder.

'You told them?'

'They tricked me.'

'You idiot. I knew I should have kept you out of it.'

'We know now, so why don't you just calm down, and tell us about the phone,' suggested Norman.

Tim muttered and cursed for a couple of minutes before he eventually calmed down.

'The night of the accident I was watching from the top of the bank. I saw this man moving the girl, and then he took a few steps away from the car. He seemed to have something in his hand. I didn't know what it was at the time, but he did something with it that I couldn't see, then he threw one part to his right, then turned and threw the other part to his left.'

'Then what?'

'Then he ran off through the trees on the other side of the road. About five minutes later the first police car arrived. I didn't want to get involved, so I sloped off out of the way.'

'And you expect us to believe the guy was throwing the phone away, and you went back later and picked it up?' asked Slater.

'He threw the battery in one direction, and the main body of the phone in the other direction,' said Tim. 'I knew roughly where to look, but it took me weeks of searching to find both parts. It's lucky it was during a dry spell, or it might have been ruined.'

'So how come you've only just started to use it?' asked Norman.

'I know it's hard to believe,' said Tim, sarcastically, 'but there's not much call for a mobile phone when you have no friends, no money and no electricity. I dunno why I bothered finding it really. Curiosity I suppose. But even then, once I had it, I had no idea what to do with it, so I just kept it.'

'You could have given it to the police.'

'People like me try not to get involved in anything that might lead to us having to explain who we are, or how we come to know something. The idea is to stay below the radar as much as possible.'

'Stay invisible, right?' asked Norman.

'Exactly!'

'So what changed recently to make you decide to get the phone working?' asked Slater.

'How do you mean?'

'Even if the phone itself were still in working order, the battery would have been dead. And Lilly's account was closed so the SIM would have been useless. That means you would have needed to charge the battery and get a new SIM card for it. For a man out here in the middle of nowhere, that's a lot of trouble to go to, so I figure there must have been a good reason.'

'Not really.'

'Who helped you get it going?' Slater turned to Sellars. 'I assume it was you, was it?'

Kelly looked at Tim, then shook his head.

'I didn't even know he had a phone until a couple of weeks ago.'

Slater turned back to Tim. 'What about the SIM card? Where did that come from?'

'That young Mickey saw me messing about with it. He gave me one of those Pay As You Go cards. He said there was £10 credit on it for me to use.'

'Did he charge the battery for you?'

'He took it home one night, and then brought it back the next day, fully charged.'

'He thought you were going to use it?'

'Yes, I suppose he did, but I just wanted to see if there was anything of interest on the phone.'

'Was there?'

'I thought so.'

'Where is the phone now?'

'It was good of the boy to think of me and help me get it working, but who am I going to call? I don't have any use for it, so I gave it back to him and told him to keep it.'

Slater glanced at Norman.

'So, you're telling me you went to all the trouble of getting the phone working, and then you gave it to Mickey?'

'Why is that a problem?' asked Tim. 'He's a nice kid, and it was his girlfriend's old phone. It seemed only right to give it to him.'

'You're sure he's a nice kid, are you?' asked Slater. 'Only it looks to me as if he must be the one who sent a malicious text to his dead girl-friend's mother.'

'Ah, yes, about that,' said Tim. 'It wasn't Mickey, it was me.'

'Why?' asked Norman. 'You've lost a daughter of your own. How d'you think the poor woman felt when that message appeared on her phone?'

Tim looked suitably guilty.

'It was an accident,' he said. 'The message had been written but not sent. I haven't used a mobile phone in years. They're a little more advanced these days. I sent it by mistake.'

Slater looked at him in disbelief.

'By mistake?'

'I meant to delete it, but I pressed the wrong button. It was a genuine mistake. Believe me, I feel terrible about it, but you can't undo these things can you?'

Slater studied his face.

'I'm not sure I can believe you,' he said, finally. 'You've fed us so many lies already, this is probably just another one to add to the list. I dare say if we come back tomorrow you'll give us another version of events.'

Tim stared back at Slater, with a cheeky grin on his face, but he said nothing. Norman could see Tim was ramping up the tension, seeing how far he could push Slater.

'I think we're probably done here for now,' said Norman, 'but don't be surprised if we're back real soon.'

'I'll look forward to it,' said Tim.

'C'mon, Dave, let's get out here,' said Norman.

Slater gave Tim one last glare, then spun on his heel and followed Norman.

'So that's something else Mickey's mother doesn't know,' said Norman as they climbed back into their car.

'D'you mean about him being friends with Tim, or about him having Lilly's mobile phone?'

Norman laughed. 'Yeah. For a son who tells his mother everything there seems to be a lot of stuff she's completely unaware of.'

'Did you think that was the real deal we just heard or were we just being fed more bullshit?' asked Slater.

'You mean from Tim? It's hard to tell,' said Norman. 'I think he lives in a different reality to the rest of us. In his world truth seems to be flexible and adjustable.'

'So you thought it was bullshit, too?'

Norman pulled a face.

'Some of it was undoubtedly crap, but some of it was equally plausible.'

'There's something about him I really don't get,' said Slater. 'If he's so determined to kill Jason Crothers, what's he doing camped out in that old car? He knows the guy doesn't live here, so what's he waiting for?'

'He said he's only just found that out and Kelly sort of confirmed it.'

'I'm not sure I believe that,' said Slater. 'And don't forget Kelly's his brother and seems quite happy to be going along with this plan to kill Crothers. On that basis, I take everything he says with a huge pinch of salt.'

'Whatever,' said Norman, wearily. 'To tell the truth, I've just about had enough for one day. Let's go and talk to Lizzie Becker, then go home.'

'Suits me,' said Slater, putting the car into gear and pulling away.

They drove on in an unusually gloomy silence for a few minutes.

'Are you okay, Norm?'

'Who me? Yeah, sure.'

'Only you're very quiet. It's not like you.'

'No, really. Don't worry about me. I'm just peachy.'

'Are you sure? Only the words and voice thing tells me differently,' said Slater.

'Words and voice thing?'

'Your words and your body language. They aren't saying the same thing.'

'No, really, I'm fine. I have a headache, and I'm a bit tired, that's all. I haven't been sleeping well.'

'Something on your mind?'

'Nothing I wanna share.'

'Oh, right. Pardon me for asking,' said Slater, sulkily.

'I didn't mean it like that,' said Norman. 'What I mean is I'm fine. I don't want to share because I have nothing on my mind to share.'

Slater was unconvinced, but he respected Norman's desire to keep his problem to himself.

'Just remember I'm here if you need anything, right?'

'Yeah, I know that, and I appreciate it,' said Norman, 'but honestly I'm just tired.'

24

Lizzie Becker was pleased to see them on her doorstep and quick to invite them in.

'Have you found out who sent the text message?' she asked.

'We're not sure yet,' said Norman, 'but we are getting nearer. We do know it was sent from Lilly's old phone.'

'Really? It's turned up after all this time? How can you be sure it's her phone? Where was it?'

'We know it was sent from Lilly's phone because every mobile phone has this inbuilt ID number. As for where it's been, we're working on a couple of possible theories.'

'Like what?'

'It's possible someone may have taken it from the crash site before the police arrived.'

'You mean someone came across the accident, stopped to steal the phone and then drove off? That's terrible!'

'It's just a theory,' said Norman. 'Of course, it may not be quite that bad. It could be that the phone was thrown clear of the crash and found a few days later.'

'The police said that was unlikely,' said Lizzie. 'They said they searched for a hundred yards back down the road.'

'There is one other possibility,' said Slater.

'You mean—'

'There could have been someone in the car with her.'

Lizzie's eyes widened.

'Now look, we don't want to get your hopes up,' said Norman. 'We think it's a possibility, but we're a long way from proving it.'

'You're talking about a driver?'

'Possible driver,' said Slater.

'But why do you think that? I always said as much, but the police were adamant...'

'It's a work in progress,' said Norman. 'But we think if we can find the phone we might just be able to prove it.'

'Oh my goodness, that would be wonderful.'

'But we need your help,' said Norman.

'How can I help?'

'Well, it's little awkward, but we know someone who managed to get access to Lilly's post mortem report.'

Lizzie seemed to shrink into her seat, and she looked down at her hands.

'Ah. I see.'

'It seems Lilly was...' began Norman. 'What I mean is... er, Jeez, this is difficult.'

Lizzie suddenly sat up straight and looked him in the eye.

'You mean, did I know Lilly was having sex with someone?'

Norman's mouth dropped open.

'Er, yeah. The report says Lilly was sexually active, although she hadn't been on that day.'

Lizzie sighed.

'Yes, I did know.'

'Do you know who with?'

'I assumed it was Mickey. He was the only boy I knew she spent any time with.'

'Did you actually ask her?' asked Slater.

'When I say I knew, what I mean is, I suspected.'

'So you didn't actually ask?'

'Do you know what it's like to have a teenage daughter, Mr Slater?'

'No, I don't have any children.'

'She was all I had after my husband died,' Lizzie was sobbing now. 'We were very close, she was like my best friend. I wanted to ask her about it, but I couldn't risk alienating her. She was all I had!'

It was a good half an hour before Lizzie had recovered enough to convince them it was okay to leave her.

'That was tough,' said Norman, as Slater drove away from her house.

'Yeah, it was. I didn't realise she'd lost her husband as well. That's really grim, losing both of them.'

'It makes you want to try and do something to help,' said Norman.

'Well, we can't bring Lilly back, but maybe if we prove she wasn't alone in that car, we can at least restore her good name. That might help.'

'You think it's Mickey, don't you?'

'He's got to be the favourite, hasn't he?'

'He has an alibi, you know. He was with his mother.'

'Everybody has an alibi,' said Slater. 'D'you think his mother would lie for him?'

Norman sighed.

'Honestly? Yeah, I think she would.'

'Did she?'

'I'm happy to go and ask her,' said Norman, 'but can it wait until the morning? My head feels like it's going to burst.'

'Sure. I'll take you back to the office, and you can get off home.'

25

It was 9 am, and Slater's phone was ringing.

'Stella! This is unexpected. Are you okay?'

'Yes, I'm fine. It's just that I've got an opportunity to do some real police work for a change, and... Can we take a rain check tonight?'

'You not going out on an operation, are you?'

'Ha! I wish. No, there's a surveillance job on tonight, and they've asked me to coordinate from here. I think it might be some sort of test, but I don't care, it's been such a long time since I did real police work. Say you don't mind.'

'Of course, I don't mind. I've got plenty to catch up on the case here anyway.'

'Talking about that, I have some information for you.'

'Go on.'

'There's no-one called Josh Ludlow working for Keeling Security.'

'No surprise there. We didn't think there would be, but at least now we know for sure.'

'There is something else I found curious, though. They have a guy called Kenneth Pearce working as an installation engineer. He started about eighteen months ago.'

'And?'

'Kenny Pearce has a record, for breaking and entering.'

'You know what they say about using a poacher as a gamekeeper.'

'Yes, but this is a security business. They shouldn't be employing a guy like that. If he's installing security systems, he'll have a damned good idea what's in those houses, and he'll know how to disable their security systems.'

'I see what you mean, but I don't see how it affects our case.'

'Maybe it doesn't, but did you know Kenny Pearce provided Jason Crothers' alibi the night Lilly Becker died? The story is they were both staying in the same hotel in Norfolk, and they ended up playing snooker all night.

'Really? Now that might be worth knowing.'

Voices could be heard in the background.

'Sorry, I've got to go,' said Stella. 'I'll speak to you tomorrow.'

'Yeah, sure.'

Absently, Slater put his phone down and wondered about this new information. His gut was telling him it was important, but... His thoughts were interrupted by Norman blundering through the door. His clothes looked as if he'd slept in them, but his face looked as if he hadn't slept at all.

'Jesus, Norm,' began Slater.

'Yeah, I'm sorry I'm late. I overslept.'

Norman's mouth opened in a huge yawn which one hand did nothing to hide.

'Overslept? You look as if you haven't slept at all! What's going on?'

'I'm okay,' said Norman. 'I just need coffee.'

'You'd better sit down,' said Slater, his concern loud and clear. 'I'll get you some coffee.'

'OKAY,' said Norman, after half a cup of coffee. 'I'm ready to rock and roll.'

'Are you sure you're okay?'

'Never felt better,' said Norman, unconvincingly. 'My head was busting yesterday, but I'm fine now. So, what's the plan?'

'I was just speaking to Stella before you came in. There is no-one called Josh Ludlow working for Keeling Security.'

'Yeah, well, we kinda guessed the guy wasn't real, didn't we? I don't know about you, but I've had enough of everyone lying all the time. It's high time we started making some waves to get some of these people to tell us the truth. Why don't we start with Summer Duval?'

'Okay, but while you finish your coffee, there's something else that might interest you.'

'Sure, let's hear it.'

'According to Stella, Keeling Security employ a guy called Kenny Pearce as an installation engineer.'

'Why would that interest me?'

'Because Kenny Pearce has a conviction for breaking and entering and because Kenny provided Jason Crothers with an alibi the night Lilly Becker died.'

Norman scratched his head.

'I'm still not feeling a great deal of interest.'

'If Jason Crothers and Kenny Pearce were in Norfolk that night, presumably they were working up there. If they worked together, were they friends? If so, were they close enough friends to lie for each other?'

'Well, yeah, I guess they could have been, but I thought we fancied Mickey as the phantom car driver.'

'But we should check this guy out right, I mean—' Slater stopped mid-sentence. 'No, wait! They couldn't have been working together. Stella said Pearce had worked for Keeling Security for eighteen months, but Lilly died two years ago!'

'Maybe they were working together, but unofficially,' suggested Norman.

'How d'you mean?'

'Didn't you say there were two complaints about Jason Crothers arriving just after people's houses had been broken into? What if that's the scam? Crothers finds the target, Pearce breaks in, and then a couple of days later Crothers turns up selling a security system. How neat is that?'

'It's pretty cute, isn't it?' said Slater. 'D'you think Malcolm Keeling knows about it?'

'Now wouldn't that be something? They say the guy's an innovator, perhaps this is his innovative client recruitment system.'

'But then, maybe he didn't know. Perhaps that's why Keeling gave Jason the old heave-ho. Perhaps he found out about the scam.'

'But if that's the case, why keep using him? And why employ Pearce?'

Slater scratched his head.

'Perhaps Pearce demanded a job in return for his silence. I mean, if it got out Malcolm Keeling was using a scam to grow his business...'

Norman nodded.

'Okay, so we think Keeling uses a scam to get business, but that's not our problem is it? The police can deal with that. How does it help us?'

'If Crothers doesn't have an alibi, he could have been the driver.'

Norman pulled a face.

'I'm not sure he's in the frame, but then I suppose we can't rule him out for sure. On that basis I guess it wouldn't hurt to test his alibi, just to make sure.' He rubbed his hands together. 'Okay, so where do we start?'

'I thought we could start with Summer Duval,' said Slater, 'and then get this Josh Ludlow thing sorted. After what Lizzie said yesterday, we also need to check out Mickey's alibi. And I think we need to find Kenny Pearce and speak to him.'

'I think we need to speak to Malcolm Keeling as well,' said Norman. 'I'm not sure how this security scam fits in with our case, but I have a feeling he knows a lot more than he's told us so far.'

'That's a lot of people to speak to,' said Slater.

'We'd better get started then.'

26

The broad smile on Summer Duval's face disappeared as soon as she saw who was standing on her doorstep.

'Oh. You two again,' she said, looking down on them. 'I thought we agreed you wouldn't come back.'

'Hey look,' said Norman, 'we've come nice and early during the day to make sure your husband doesn't see us.'

'You shouldn't be here at all. We agreed—'

'We agreed we wouldn't come back as long as you didn't send us off with a crock full of shit,' said Norman. 'Unfortunately, you didn't keep your side of the deal.'

'Oh, yes I did. I gave you a bloody name.'

'You mean Josh Ludlow? That was the part that was bullshit. What did you do? Stick a pin in a map and choose the nearest town as a surname? We need a real name, not something you made up on the spur of the moment.'

'But that's the name he gave me.'

'What does this guy look like?' asked Slater, pulling the photograph of Jason Crothers from his pocket. 'Is this him?'

She rolled her eyes and gave him a look of sympathy.

'Really?' she said, without bothering to look at the photo. 'You think I meet these people in person?' She turned to Norman. 'Are you sure your friend's a detective?'

Norman couldn't help but grin. She was right, it had been a pretty dumb question, and out of the corner of his eye he could see Slater realised it, too.

'Okay,' said Norman. 'So you've never seen the guy, but you must have spoken to him. What does he sound like?'

'Well, I don't know. Like a bloke, of course.'

'Come on, Summer,' urged Norman. 'If you don't want to have to explain to your husband why two guys are standing on your doorstep when he gets home, you need to start being a bit more helpful.'

'You'll have a long wait,' she jeered. 'He won't be home for hours yet.'

'That's okay. We have nowhere to rush off to,' said Norman, with a wicked grin.

'You wouldn't.'

'D'you really want to find out?'

She sighed her frustration. She had met detectives like Norman before, in a previous life. She had no doubt he would do as promised if she didn't co-operate.

'I moved here to get away from people like you,' she hissed.

'I bet you never told your husband what you used to do, right? So he has no idea.'

A look of alarm flashed across her face.

'So, I got that right, huh?' asked Norman.

'I did what I had to do to get by,' she snapped. 'Anyway, that was a long time ago.'

'Now calm down,' said Norman. 'That wasn't a threat. Trust me we all have a past, and we're not going to tell anyone about yours. But I have to warn you we're getting pissed off with people telling us lies. We could change our minds if we don't get some help real soon.'

She sighed again.

'Why are you protecting him?' asked Norman.

'Because he's a customer,' she snapped.

'D'you honestly think he would protect you if the situation were reversed?' asked Norman.

She didn't say anything for a few seconds, so Norman offered some encouragement.

'Of course, if you'd rather we wait for your husband...'

'You know what?' she said. 'Now I think about it, I am fed up having to deal with calls from his girlfriend. I keep giving him the messages but I'm sure he never calls her back, and all I get is more and more earache from her. I keep telling her it's not my fault he doesn't call her back, but I'm sure she doesn't believe me. Yeah, sod it, why should I protect him?'

'That's my girl,' encouraged Norman. 'Now you're beginning to speak our language.'

'I still don't see how I can help though. I already told you Josh Ludlow was the name he gave me, and I've never met him. I know nothing about him.'

'Is Josh Ludlow the name callers ask for on that line?' asked Norman.

'Look, I don't ask questions,' she said. 'I take the message, and when someone calls to pick it up, I pass the message on. There could be calls coming in for a dozen different people on one number.'

'But you speak to one person collecting calls for that number, right?' asked Slater.

She nodded.

'And that person calls himself Josh Ludlow?'

'Yes, that's right.'

'So you know his voice,' said Slater. 'Or are you suggesting every man sounds identical?'

She looked daggers at him, but Slater just grinned.

'Of course, they don't all sound the same,' she said. 'I just don't take a lot of notice.'

'Come on, Summer, you can do better than that,' he said. 'Think! Does he have an accent? Is he softly spoken? Does he shout? There must be something you can tell us.'

'Yeah, that's it,' she said, looking pleased with herself. 'Now you mention it, I remember. He has got a bit of an accent.'

'What sort of an accent?' asked Norman.

'I dunno,' she said. 'I'm not very good with accents.'

'Is it Northern? Cockney? Foreign?'

'I'm not sure you'd call it foreign,' she said, vaguely. 'Maybe Scottish, or Irish, or something like that anyway.'

'Now we're getting somewhere,' said Norman.

'I don't think I can tell you anything else.'

Norman looked at Slater.

'I suppose what we've got is better than nothing,' he said.

'It's a bit more than we knew before,' agreed Slater.

'Is that it?' asked Summer. 'Will you clear off now?'

'Yeah, we'll clear off now,' said Norman. 'But before we go could I ask one more thing?'

'Oh gawd, now what?' she asked, impatient to have them gone.

'Can you let me have the name of that girlfriend trying to get hold of him?'

'Wait here. I'll write it down for you.'

She stepped back into the hall where she found a small notebook in a drawer, wrote down the name, tore out the page, folded it in half, then came back and handed it to Norman.

'If you speak to her,' she said, 'can you tell her to stop calling me, and to stop wasting her time chasing after him. He's never going to call her back. She should have realised that by now.'

'Yeah, I'll give her your message.'

'I hope this is the last time I'm going to see you two,' she said.

'Trust me, the feeling's mutual,' said Norman.

Across the road, half a dozen houses down, a nosey neighbour had been watching the proceedings on Summer's doorstep. Now as the boys turned away, she gave the neighbour a very deliberate, heartfelt, two-fingered salute.

'Seen enough?' she called across the road.

The neighbour hurried inside. Summer stepped back into her own house and slammed the door.

. . .

'AT LEAST NOW WE know something about Jason Crothers,' said Norman when they were back in the car. 'We now know he speaks with a bit of an accent.'

'That's if you can believe anything she said,' muttered Slater as he pulled away down the road. 'And I still can't believe that's her real name. I mean, come on, Summer Duval? Really?'

Sitting next to him, Norman unfolded the sheet of paper he had been given and let out a long whistle.

'You want an exotic name?' he said. 'How about Rosabella Rizzi? Is that exotic enough for you?'

'Wow! She sounds like an Italian porn star. I wonder what she can tell us about this mess.'

'I'll ask her, shall I?'

Slater glanced from the road to Norman.

'And how are you going to do that?'

'Let's go back to the office, and I'll find her number. It won't be that difficult. I mean there can't be that many Rosabella Rizzi's, can there?'

27

'Jeez, my ears are ringing,' said Norman, as he walked into Slater's office. 'Italian may well be one of the romantic languages, but when that woman speaks, it's also one of the scariest.'

Slater turned and smiled.

'You got hold of her, then?'

'With a name like Rosabella, I had this mental image of a dark, sultry, softly spoken, latin beauty. The reality is she sounds like a bloody harpy. I wouldn't want to be in that guy's shoes if she ever gets her hands on him. He sure won't be fathering any more kids, and I have no idea what some of those Italian curses meant!'

'Did you actually find out what he did to upset her so much?'

'When she eventually calmed down and stopped the ranting, she told me she met him two years ago after she had a security system installed and then suffered a burglary. He went to her house to offer his apologies and ended up suggesting an upgrade to their security system. An affair ensued, and he promised to leave his wife for her, but then he started showing an unhealthy interest in her teenage daughter. This made her so jealous she kicked him out but then, shortly afterwards he started blackmailing her. He told her if she didn't order an upgrade to the security system he would tell her husband all about their affair.'

'And did she order the upgrade?'

'About a year ago. She paid five grand for it.'

'I take it she's not seen him since she handed over the money?'

'That's right, but I couldn't decide if she was more upset about losing the money, or just plain jealous of her beautiful daughter catching his eye.'

'So what do we think? Is this guy a conman?'

'No, he's a philandering conman,' said Norman. 'And Ms Rizzi has offered us a lot of money if we can lead her to him.'

Slater laughed.

'We could do with the money, but not if we're going to get charged with being accessories to murder.'

'I think that's a distinct possibility,' said Norman.

'We suspect Mia Crothers knew about her husband's affair with Keira Silver, right? I wonder if she also knew about Rosabella Rizzi,' said Slater.

'D'you think?'

'Maybe she was prepared to accept the first one, but the second was too much to bear.'

'I guess it would explain why she doesn't want to speak to him,' said Norman, 'but if it's that bad, why not divorce him?'

'Maybe it's because all the time she stays married he keeps her in the style she's accustomed to.'

'That's a very cynical point of view.'

'Yeah, but it's probably true, isn't it?' said Slater.

'I'm afraid it probably is, sad, but true,' agreed Norman. He thought for a minute or two. 'Okay, then, here's a thought; when we spoke to her, Mia Crothers seemed to think Jason was still working for Keeling Security. Do you think she was for real, and she doesn't know he's not there anymore?'

'If you mean, does she know she's being supported by a conman? I don't know. I'd like to think she's got enough moral fibre not to live that way, but something about her didn't ring true, did it? Then again, she did give us his card.'

'D'you think she may have done that on purpose so we could expose him?' asked Norman.

'Either that, or she's hoping we can find him.'

'So why doesn't she go to the police?'

Slater spread his arms.

'Because then she might have to admit she knew what he was up to?' he guessed. 'I don't know. Maybe I'm wrong, and she really doesn't know he's not with Keeling anymore.'

'But surely she would have contacted them looking for him?' asked Norman.

Slater shrugged.

'I dunno, Norm,' he said. 'The whole thing seems a bit of a weird setup to me, even if they are separated. What must the son think?'

'Yeah, if he's been living in a family environment like that it makes you wonder how he's going to grow up, doesn't it?'

The phone was ringing out in Norman's office.

'I'm going to have that phone moved into your office,' he muttered as he headed back to his desk.

'Yo!' said Norman into his phone.

'Er, is that Mr Norman? Norman Norman?'

'That's me. Who wants to know?'

'My name is Keira Silver. We spoke the other day briefly.'

Norman nearly fell off his chair.

'Keira. Wow! This is a surprise. How did you get my number?'

'We keep visitor logs at Keeling Security.'

'You found our names and looked up the number?'

'Yes, that's right.'

'Okay Keira, what can I do for you?'

. . .

'I'VE JUST HAD Keira Silver on the phone,' said Norman a couple of minutes later. 'She wants to speak to us.'

'I thought she was forbidden from speaking to anyone.'

'Yeah, that's right. For that reason, she won't let us go anywhere near Keeling Security, but she definitely wants to see us. She says she thinks we need to hear what she has to say about Jason Crothers.'

'Okay, where and when?'

'She has a day off, and she's in Tinton. She'll be here in a few minutes!'

'She's keen, isn't she?'

'Are you complaining?'

'Heck, no, it beats trying to track people down.'

The sound of the outside door opening stopped them in their tracks.

'That'll be her now,' said Norman, and headed for the front office, Slater hot on his heels.

28

At first, Slater thought they had been mistaken. What appeared to be a teenager was standing just inside the door, fidgeting nervously from foot to foot.

'My name's Keira Silver,' she said.

Slater managed to hide his surprise, but Norman's face gave him away immediately.

'You look surprised,' she said. 'I did say I was just down the road.'

'I'm sorry,' said Norman. 'It's just that I was expecting someone older. You're just a t-'

'No,' she said. 'I'm forty-four. I have a daughter of fifteen. I've always looked like a kid. Some people think I'm lucky. Personally, I think it's a curse when no-one takes you seriously.'

Slater thought Keira would make a gorgeous teenager, but he could understand why she felt cursed. He supposed youthful good looks were probably something most people craved, but she looked just a little bit too young. He could understand what she meant about not being taken seriously.

'Can I ask why you've decided to come forward now?' he asked. 'I thought speaking out was forbidden.'

'It is. You need to understand, if Malcolm ever finds out I've spoken to you, I'll lose my job,' she said. 'It's hard enough raising a teenager on my own, without that.'

'So what's changed?'

'I'm not quite sure what's going on at the office, but it's as if there's some sort of panic on.'

Norman looked at Slater.

'Stella must have rattled his cage,' mumbled Slater.

'I'm sorry?' said Keira.

'It's nothing for you to worry about,' said Slater. 'Please carry on.'

She hesitated briefly, then continued.

'Malcolm's been running around screaming at people, and every trace of Jason Crothers is being removed. The paper shredder is working overtime. I got the distinct impression yesterday afternoon we might all be about to lose our jobs. It made me wonder if keeping quiet is the right thing to do.'

'You know why Jason was fired, don't you, Keira?' asked Norman.

'If this ever gets back...'

'Anything you say to us, stays with us,' said Norman. 'Why don't you come and sit down?'

He led her across the room, settled her in a chair, and he and Slater sat around her.

'Okay,' said Norman. 'You said you wanted to tell us about Jason Crothers. Well, you have our attention. We're all ears.'

'Jason was my boss,' she began. 'At first everything was very business-like, but gradually he became a little less formal, and eventually, he started telling me how unhappy he was at home.

Then, one day he took me out to lunch. To my surprise, he was very charming and treated me like a proper lady. No-one had ever treated me like that before. I was on my own, I was lonely, and well, one thing led to another. Before I knew it, we were having an affair.'

'When did this start?' asked Norman.

'The affair started about two years ago, just after his car got smashed up. He told me that car was the only joy he had in life. He was so upset when it happened. I suppose I felt sorry for him.'

Slater was wondering why Malcolm Keeling would have considered an office affair such a big deal it had to be kept secret.

'So why did the relationship end?' asked Norman.

'It was wonderful at first. As I said, Jason treated me like a lady, but then he changed.'

'In what way?'

'He started buying me clothes and stuff.'

'And that was a problem because your husband wanted to know where it was coming from?'

'No. I was already divorced back then. It was a problem because the clothes weren't really for me. I had told him my daughter used to borrow my clothes. We were the same size, you see.'

Slater felt his skin begin to crawl.

'My daughter was just thirteen at the time. He met her once, and she was wearing something he had bought for me. He got really excited about that. It was disgusting and frightening, very frightening.'

'I can imagine that must have been pretty scary,' said Norman. 'What did you do?'

'I kicked him out of my house, and told him never to come near me, or my daughter, again.'

'That must have made things a bit awkward at work.'

'We had a big row. He told me I was just a cheap slut. He even said he was only attracted to me in the first place because I looked like an adolescent.'

'What happened after that?'

'I told Diana Williams everything. She told Malcolm Keeling, and Jason Crothers was gone the same day.'

'He must have been mad about that,' said Norman. 'Has he been in contact with you since?'

'He tried to speak to my daughter once, after school, but she ran back into the school and hid. That was the last time.'

'Let me get this straight,' said Norman. 'You're saying he's attracted to little girls?'

'Not really little girls. Early teens, thirteen, fourteen, that seems to be his thing.'

'Did you report this to the police?'

'I was going to, but Malcolm said not to. He didn't want the company name smeared with something like that.'

'So, you know there's a pervert out there, and you did nothing about it?'

She looked stunned.

'But Malcolm said not to. I didn't have a choice. I could have lost my job!'

'How are you going to feel if a young girl loses her life at the hands of Jason Crothers?' asked Slater.

Keira's hand shot to her mouth.

'He hasn't, has he?'

'We don't know,' said Slater. 'But what you've just told us makes it a possibility.'

'Oh my God. D'you think I should have gone to the police?'

'I don't think you need us to tell you what you should have done.'

'What about my job?'

'I thought you said it looked as though you were going to lose that anyway,' said Slater. 'Isn't that why you're here?'

'Oh, God. What should I do?'

Norman shrugged. 'You have to do what you think is right.'

'Here's the number of a Detective Inspector you could speak to,' said Slater, writing a number down on his pad. He tore the sheet of paper from his notepad and handed it to her. 'Her name is Stella Robbins.'

'I FEEL SICK,' said Slater, after Keira had left.

'Me too,' said Norman.

'If what we just heard is true this guy Crothers is dangerous.'

'Yeah, I don't think there's any doubt about that.'

'Can you get hold of that Italian woman again?'

'You mean Rosabella?'

'Yeah, that's the one. Didn't she say something about her daughter? Find out how old she is.'

'You can see the same pattern as me?' asked Norman.

'Keira's daughter was thirteen, and Lilly was fourteen. Frankly, that's good enough for me, but if your Italian lady says her daughter is fifteen or sixteen now, well...'

'Does this mean you're no longer convinced Mickey was driving the night Lilly died?'

'It means I think it's highly unlikely, don't you?'

TEN MINUTES later Norman confirmed their worst fears.

'Rosabella Rizzi says her daughter has just turned sixteen.'

'Shit!' said Slater. 'Shit, shit, shit!'

'This guy sounds like a predator,' said Norman.

'I think he was the one having sex with Lilly.'

'It has to be considered a distinct possibility,' agreed Norman.

'And here's another thing,' said Slater. 'If Mia Crothers knew about it, it might explain why she kicked Jason out, and why she hates Lilly so much.'

'You're right,' agreed Norman. 'All of a sudden a lot of things start to fall into place. There's just one problem, though. Jason Crothers has an alibi for the night of the accident.'

'Right. So we need to find Kenny Pearce and put this alibi to the test. We also need to carry on where we left off this morning and speak to Malcolm Keeling and Mia Crothers.'

'We need to find out if they knew about his preferences.'

'I can't believe his wife didn't know,' said Slater. 'It explains why she kicked him out but didn't file for divorce. I wouldn't be surprised if that's the hold she has over him. He pays, or she talks.'

'It figures,' agreed Norman. 'But where do we go first? What if they both know? And another thing, should we tell the police? I mean this isn't just about who sent a text message anymore. If we're right, this is a serious sex offender we're talking about. We can't handle something like that on our own. You'd better call Stella and tell her what we know.'

Slater frowned.

'We'll lose our case. They're certain to tell us to stop interfering.'

Norman smiled and winked.

'They'll tell us to stop interfering in the pervert case, but that's okay, we're not going to get paid for that anyway. In the meantime, we still have to find out who sent that text message, and we have to find a missing son.'

Now Slater smiled, too.

'And it just so happens we have to find the pervert, to find the missing son.'

'Exactly,' said Norman.

'I'll make that call.'

29

Unlike Summer Duval the previous morning, Mia Crothers was delighted to find Norman standing on her doorstep.

'Why, Norman, what a nice surprise! You should have called to say you were on the way.'

She beamed a huge smile in Norman's direction, but it rapidly faded when she saw Slater walking over to join him.

'Oh. You're here, too.'

Slater aimed his best smile at her.

'Good morning, Mrs Crothers. It's nice to see you, too.'

'We're sorry to come unannounced, Mia,' said Norman. 'Only something's just come up, and we wondered if you could help us.'

'As it's you, I'll help if I can,' she said. 'But I have to warn you if your friend had come alone I would not have opened the door.'

Slater nodded enthusiastically but kept his mouth firmly closed.

'Yeah, I think we understand that,' said Norman.

'What can I help you with?'

'Can you tell us where Mickey was at the time of the accident?'

A look of horror crossed her face.

'You can't be serious,' she said. 'He was just a boy of fourteen.'

'With respect Mrs Crothers,' said Slater. 'Lilly Becker was just a girl of fourteen.'

'Don't you try to compare my son with that girl,' she hissed. 'She was—'

'I think you already made it quite clear what you thought of Lilly,' said Norman, tersely. 'We hardly need to hear it again. Perhaps you could just answer the question, and then we'll get out of your hair.'

The look of utter distaste that filled her face told Norman what she thought of this apparent betrayal of their friendship.

'Mickey was with me when the accident happened,' she hissed, through clenched teeth.

Slater sighed. This was like drawing teeth.

'As my colleague just suggested, the sooner you answer the question, the sooner we'll leave.'

'I have answered the question.'

'Perhaps if you could give us a little more detail...'

'It was my birthday on 14th February, and it was a half-term week. We have a holiday cottage in the New Forest. As a treat, Mickey and I went down there. We left here on Saturday morning, and we were due to return on the following Saturday. Of course, in the event, our week away was ruined, and we had to come back early.'

Slater let out an involuntary snort of disgust. Her eyes widened, and she looked daggers at him.

'Is there a problem?' she asked.

'Don't you feel any sympathy for Lilly Becker or her family?' asked Norman. 'I understood you were family friends and your kids had grown up together.'

'We were family friends until that girl showed what she really thought about friendship and trust.'

She spoke as if the very thought of mentioning Lilly's name would somehow make her dirty.

'Didn't you ever make mistakes when you were young?' asked Slater.

'Of course, I did, but never on that scale!'

Slater and Norman shared a look. It was clear there was nothing to be gained by further exploration of Mia Crothers' hate-filled view of Lilly Becker.

'And you're quite sure Mickey was with you the whole time?' asked Slater. 'He couldn't have slipped out for a few hours?'

'Of course, he wouldn't leave me alone on my birthday. What a thing to suggest.'

'Alone? You mean your husband wasn't with you? I thought you separated a few months later.'

'My husband was working, as usual,' she said. 'He rarely had time for me, even on my birthday.'

'I don't suppose you know where he was?'

'I think it was Norfolk, but you will have to check with him.'

'Yeah, we will, when we find him,' said Norman.

'I thought you said having Mickey's mobile phone number would allow you to track him.'

'We can only track the phone if he switches it on,' said Norman. 'So far he hasn't obliged.'

'Can I ask what car your husband drives?' asked Slater.

'The last time I saw him, he was driving a Mercedes four-wheel drive thing, and no, I don't know the model or the registration number.'

She made to close the door, but Slater hadn't finished yet.

'I don't suppose you'd like to give us the address of the cottage you and Mickey—'

'No, I will not,' she snapped, impatiently. 'I think I've had enough of your impertinence and accusations.'

Now she addressed Norman directly.

'You have the potential to be a nice man, Norman.' She cast a look of disgust in Slater's direction. 'I don't understand why you associate with this person, but if you take my advice, you'll find yourself a new partner.'

'It's very good of you to offer your advice about my potential,' said Norman. 'The thing is I've never been very good at taking unwanted advice, and I'm a bit long in the tooth to start doing it now. I can assure you I have no intention of changing my partner, and I'll thank you to keep your advice to yourself.'

Mia Crothers looked as if someone had just slapped her face.

'How dare you speak to me like that?'

'Oh, it's quite easy,' said Norman.

Her eyes were becoming impossibly wide.

'What?' asked Norman. 'D'you think you're so special you have the right to tell me how to live my life?'

'I think you should leave, right now!'

'Don't worry, we're going,' said Norman. 'The atmosphere here is much too bitter. It's making me feel ill.'

There was a loud crash as the door slammed. Norman thought about hammering on it and continuing the argument. He was in the mood. He began to reach forward, but as if he had read Norman's mind, Slater put a hand on his arm.

'Come on, mate, let's go. You don't want to waste your time arguing with someone like her.'

Reluctantly Norman turned and allowed Slater to shepherd him back to the car. He kept quiet until they were back on the road.

'Just how bitter and twisted can one woman be?' he said. 'It's not as if it was the end of the world. It was just a damned car, and it would have been insured, for Christ's sake!'

'I know what you mean,' agreed Slater. 'It seems disproportionate to hate someone that much over a stolen car. She doesn't have an ounce of sympathy for Lilly's family.'

'So, what do you think is behind it? Why is Mia Crothers so angry?'

'That's the real question, isn't it?' said Slater. 'D'you think she was telling the truth about Mickey being with her all the time?'

'She was adamant he was there.'

'Yeah, but I thought she was just a bit too adamant, didn't you?'

'You think she was lying?'

'I think it's possible she's protecting him.'

'Seriously?' said Norman. 'You think she's giving Mickey an alibi?'

'I dunno. I just have this idea in my head that it wouldn't take that long to get from the New Forest to Winchester by train.'

'That would depend on where they were in the New Forest,' said Norman. 'And he would still have to get home from Winchester.'

'Less than twenty minutes by taxi,' said Slater. 'Not much more than an hour in total.'

'You really think he could have been driving that car? Why would he do that?'

'We know they grew up together, and we know Lilly was a pretty girl,' said Slater.

'But didn't Lewis Godden tell you Mickey wasn't interested in girls?'

'Yeah, he did, but it also occurred to me that Lewis might be trying to deflect us from the truth.'

'You need to make your mind up what you really think.'

'But aren't we supposed to keep open minds?'

Norman bobbed his head.

'I guess I can't argue with that,' he conceded.

'Maybe Mickey didn't see Lilly like that when they were growing up together, but he was fourteen, right? Suppose his hormones were taking charge and he was starting to see her in a different way? He knew his parents were out of the way so maybe he planned to impress Lilly with his driving skills, but he wasn't quite as clever as he thought.'

'It would need some pretty powerful hormones to make him do that,' said Norman.

'Are you kidding?' said Slater. 'Don't you remember being that age, and how some girls drove you crazy? Or, what if Lilly and Mickey were already having sex, and this idea of stealing the car while his parents were away had been planned for weeks?'

'Well, yeah, I suppose I can see what you mean about the hormones and sex, but I'm not sure I'd be driving a car at fourteen.'

'The police seem quite sure a fourteen-year-old girl was driving, so why not a fourteen-year-old boy?'

'But that means he left her to die,' said Norman. 'That's a pretty cold-hearted thing to do. I'm not sure a boy that young could do something like that, and then carry on as if nothing had happened.'

'He would have been terrified at the prospect of having to explain what he'd done. Fear can be a powerful reason to keep your mouth closed.'

'Something about this has changed after speaking to her, hasn't it?' asked Norman. 'You're quite certain Lilly wasn't driving now, aren't you?'

'Absolutely,' said Slater. 'And right now, I have Mickey as my hot favourite to be the driver. I think Lewis Godden is lying about his sexuality, and I think Mia Crothers is lying about where he was that night.'

'What happened to that "open mind" you mentioned a couple of minutes ago?'

'I didn't say I'd made my mind up who the driver was,' said Slater. 'I just said I was convinced Lilly wasn't driving, and right now Mickey's top of my list as to who was. I'm exploring possibilities based on what we know so far. Has it occurred to you that perhaps Mia found out Lilly and Mickey were lovers? Maybe she blames Lilly for corrupting her precious little boy.'

Norman nodded thoughtfully.

'I admit it would explain why she hates Lilly so much,' he agreed. 'But what about Jason Crothers? You have to admit there's something weird going on there.'

'Yeah, for sure,' said Slater. 'But maybe he's just a crook and what he's up to has nothing to do with Lilly's death.'

'Are you saying you want to forget about him?'

'Heck no,' said Slater. 'I don't want to exclude anyone yet. Mia was pretty vague about where he was. She said she "thinks he was in Norfolk". I reckon most wives would want to know for sure where their husband was if he was missing her birthday.'

'If it happened often enough maybe she stopped caring where he was,' suggested Norman.

'I guess that's possible, but I think we should focus on Jason's alibi next.'

'And how are we going to do that? If you're thinking about talking to Kenny Pearce you need to remember we have no idea where he lives.'

'That's right,' said Slater. 'But we know a man who should know.'

'You mean Malcolm Keeling?'

'That's the guy. We can ask him about Josh Ludlow at the same time.'

'If he'll speak to us at all.'

'He will if we can figure out the right approach.'

'I thought you had this all worked out,' said Norman.

'Who me? I know who I think we need to speak to, but getting them to talk is where you come in.'

'I appreciate the vote of confidence, but I've not had time to prepare anything.'

'Well then, Norm, in that case, you'd better get your thinking head on because it's only about twenty minutes from here.'

30

'Okay, I've got this,' said Norman, as Slater parked the car outside Keeling Security.

'Are you sure?'

Norman smiled, nervously.

'Piece of cake,' he said. 'But if you'd rather take the lead...'

'It's okay, Norm. I trust you. You leading works okay most times, so why change it now?'

'Great, but don't forget you're free to chip in if you want to.'

'I know. I will if I think I need to.'

Slater looked enquiringly at Norman.

'Are you okay?'

'Sure, why?'

'I dunno, it's as I said yesterday, you seem a bit off lately.'

'Not sleeping tends to mess with my routine, but I'll be fine, trust me.'

They pushed their way through the doors into the entrance atrium. Cara, the receptionist, recognised them and offered a warm smile.

'Good morning,' she said.

'Hi,' said Norman. 'We were wondering if it would be possible to speak to Malcolm Keeling?'

'I'm afraid Mr Keeling isn't here today.'

'How about Jason Crothers, is he here?'

Cara frowned. 'Didn't we establish he doesn't work here when you called the other day?'

Norman smiled.

'Oh, yeah, that's right, we did. How about Josh Ludlow? Is he here?'

'There is no Mr Ludlow—'

'It's funny that, because we keep coming across people who seem to be associated with this company, and yet when we come to speak to them we find they don't work here. Don't you think that's strange?'

Cara obviously didn't have an answer.

'Hey look, I'm not trying to upset you,' said Norman, 'but I have to confess I'm bewildered. Can we try one more name? How about Kenny Pearce? Does he work here?'

'I think I may have seen that name. I believe he's one of our engineers.'

'Oh great. That's one out of three. I don't suppose we can speak to him, can we?'

'If he is an engineer he's unlikely to be in the building, but let me see what I can do.'

Slater was impressed with Cara. Despite Norman firing names and questions at her, she managed to keep calm and remain unruffled. She even kept her smile.

'Would you like to take a seat?' she suggested. 'Perhaps I can find someone who can help you.'

'Would you do that?' said Norman. He turned to Slater. 'That would be really helpful, don't you think, Dave?'

Slater nodded. 'Yeah, that would be great.'

Cara pointed to the seating area where they waited last time, and they wandered across and sat down.

'It's a start,' said Slater. 'At least we didn't get asked to leave.'

'Yeah, so far so good. I wonder who they'll send to try to put us off.'

They didn't have to wait long to find out.

'Well, will you look at that?' said Slater. 'It's only the big boss himself!'

Norman turned to follow Slater's gaze. Sure enough, Malcolm Keeling was heading their way.

'At least he hasn't brought any security guards along to throw us out.'

'D'you think he's actually going to talk to us?'

'We'll soon find out,' said Norman, getting to his feet.

'Good morning, Mr Keeling,' he said. 'I could have sworn your receptionist told us you weren't around today.'

'She must have been mistaken,' said Keeling. 'As you can see, I'm very much here. I thought I answered all your questions last time you were here.'

Norman grimaced.

'Yeah, but you see, we like a clear stream, and I'm afraid one or two things have come up that have rather muddied the waters.'

Keeling looked them up and down.

'What things have come up?'

'D'you really want to do this out here in reception?' asked Slater.

Keeling looked around.

'Is there any reason why we shouldn't talk out here?' he asked.

Slater smiled a cold smile.

'No, it's fine, if that's what you really want. I'm sure we won't find the questions embarrassing, but it's quite possible you will.'

Keeling took another look around before he made his decision.

'You'd better follow me.'

He took them through a side door, and into a small room with four comfortable, easy chairs arranged in a circle.

'This is an interview room,' he said. 'We won't be disturbed in here. Now, what do you want?'

'We're not exactly sure what's going on with you and Jason Crothers, but we do know you lied to us,' said Norman.

Malcolm Keeling smiled without a trace of humour.

'I'm not in the habit of lying, Mr Norman. I believe I answered all your questions.'

'Then perhaps it was simply the case that you didn't tell us everything. I call that lying by omission.'

Keeling stared blankly at Norman.

'As I said, I believe I answered all your questions.'

'Fair enough,' said Norman. 'So maybe I need to ask some different questions. Is that okay?'

'Well, you're here now, and I don't suppose you're going to go away.'

Norman grinned.

'You can count on that.'

'Go on then, ask your damned questions.'

'How about we start with, what's the hold Jason Crothers has over you?'

Keeling let out a snort of derision.

'Rubbish,' he said. 'Jason doesn't have any sort of hold over me. I don't know who put that idea into your heads.'

'We didn't need anyone to suggest it,' said Norman. 'We figured it out for ourselves.'

'I think you're mistaken.'

'Really?' said Norman, feigning surprise. 'You see the thing is you fired the guy, and yet he still does consultancy work for you and uses your business card. I know you explained it last time we were here, but it seems so unusual to me, I just can't get my head around it.'

'It may seem unusual to you, but it makes perfectly good business sense to me. I have a business plan, and Jason is an important part of it. His dismissal is unfortunate, but if I use him as a consultant, it means I don't have to change the plan.'

'I guess that depends on why you fired the guy.'

Keeling smiled again.

'I'm not prepared to discuss why he was fired, but I can assure you it was absolutely nothing to do with his ability to find new clients. On that basis, why wouldn't I want to keep using him? He's very good at what he does.'

'Yeah, we'll come back to what he does in a minute,' said Norman. 'You know, I think I may be starting to understand how this works now, but I'm still worried that he's using a business card bearing your company name and yet you don't try to stop him. I can't understand why you allow that.'

Keeling frowned and looked from Norman to Slater. Slater nodded encouragingly, and smiled, but said nothing.

'I don't consider it a problem,' said Keeling, testily, 'because he's still acting on my behalf, and he's not stealing clients from me.'

'We're pretty sure he's not stealing clients, either,' said Norman. 'But he is posing as a director of your company when he isn't one. Now I call that fraud, which is an offence, but you seem to condone it. Somehow that doesn't seem to fit in with your supposedly squeaky clean business image.'

'He's using the card as a representative of my business. There's nothing fraudulent about it.'

Norman pursed his lips.

'I think you'll find that would depend on circumstances, but being as I didn't come here to argue, I'm prepared to agree it's a moot point. But while we're talking about the card, there is also an issue with the phone number.'

'What issue with the phone number?

'As you know the phone number on that card has nothing to do with your company. In fact, that number redirects to an answering service for Jason Crothers, but he never collects any of the messages that are left.'

Keeling seemed lost for words for once, so Slater took over.

'We got to wondering why he would use an answering service,' he said. 'I mean, if he's leaving those cards on your behalf, why not use your phone number?'

'I don't have to explain how I run my business to you,' snapped Keeling.

'Of course, you don't,' agreed Slater, 'but you won't find it so easy to stonewall a police investigation.'

'The police have no reason to investigate my business.'

'You're really sure about that are you?' asked Norman.

'They're going to swarm all over your business like a plague of locusts,' warned Slater, 'and that's never good for any business.'

Keeling smiled.

'You're bluffing, aren't you?' he said.

There was a short silent stand-off, and then Keeling broke into a grin.

'I thought so,' he said, grinning broadly. 'You've got nothing.' He made dismissive, shooing motions with his hands. 'I think you should leave now, don't you? Go on, run off to your police chums if you must, but isn't it an offence to waste the time of the police?'

Slater and Norman remained in their seats, unnervingly relaxed.

'Well, go on,' said Keeling, his grin faltering. 'This meeting is over, so I suggest you leave.'

'You know, you're right, we don't have anything solid yet,' said Norman, 'but you should be aware we're not going to stop looking.'

'And we won't stop until we find it, Malcolm. Is it okay if I call you Malcolm?' asked Slater. 'Or would you prefer Josh?'

Now the grin vanished from Keeling's face.

'I'm sorry?'

'Josh Ludlow.'

'Never heard of him. Who is he?'

'Oh, he's not a real person,' said Norman. 'Josh Ludlow doesn't exist. That's just the name you use when you're dealing with Summer Duval.'

'Summer who? I don't think I know that name.'

'Nice try,' said Norman, 'but I'm afraid you're not convincing anyone in this room. Summer Duval is that nice young lady who takes messages for you. She's the person you spoke to when you set the service up. She's the person you speak to on those rare occasions when you bother to check in with her.'

'At first, we thought Jason must be Josh Ludlow,' added Slater. 'But

Summer put us straight on that one. She remembered Josh had an Irish accent.'

'This is quite fascinating, but I really I have no idea what you're talking about,' said Keeling. 'I don't use an answering service.'

'How about Rosabella Rizzi?' asked Slater.

Keeling's eyes widened.

'Aha!' said Slater, triumphantly. 'You know her name, then. Summer Duval thinks she's Jason's pissed off ex-girlfriend. But I think she's more pissed off about being blackmailed into upgrading her security system. That's part of your business plan, is it? Is that what they mean when they say you're an innovator?'

Keeling was trying hard to keep his composure, but they could see he was seething underneath it all.

'I think we're done,' he hissed. 'I think you should leave now.'

'Not just yet,' said Slater. 'We haven't quite finished.'

'What?'

'Yes, there's one more thing we feel we should mention,' agreed Norman.

Keeling closed his eyes and began counting.

'Now you've mentioned that business plan of yours, I'm wondering if it was your idea, or Jason's,' said Norman.

'What the hell are you talking about now?'

'Breaking and entering.'

'I'm sorry?'

'Someone breaks into a house, and a couple of days later like magic, Jason turns up and tells the poor old householder how this wouldn't have happened if they had a Keeling Security system.'

'I have to admit it's so simple it's brilliant,' said Slater. 'Unfortunately for you, it's also illegal. D'you still think the police won't want to take a closer look at your business?'

'This is outrageous,' snapped Keeling. 'I've never heard such rubbish—'

'And it's not just about the dodgy way you find new clients, is it?' asked Slater.

Keeling's brow knitted into an angry frown. 'What?'

'You employ an engineer who has a criminal record,' said Norman. 'He was convicted of breaking and entering. Now he installs your systems in people's houses. How many of those houses have been broken into since he started working for you? I'm quite sure Rosabella Rizzi was one of his victims.'

'You're making this up,' snarled Keeling. 'My installation engineers are all hand-picked, and vet...' His voice trailed away into nothing.

'All of them are hand-picked and vetted. Is that what you were saying?' asked Norman. 'By you?'

Keeling didn't say anything.

'What about Kenny Pearce? Did you hand pick him? Did you personally vet him?'

'Jason,' said Keeling, quietly. 'Jason recommended and vetted him.'

'And you expect us to believe you didn't know about his record, or about the scam?' asked Slater. 'Come on, Keeling. Do you really think we're that stupid? You know what goes on in every part of this company. There's no way you didn't know.'

'I think you'll find the police are even more disbelieving than we are,' added Norman.

'Can't we keep them out of this?' begged Keeling. 'I'm a rich man. I can pay. I'll hire you, and put it through the company's books.'

'I'll tell you what you can do,' suggested Slater. 'You can tell us where we can find Jason Crothers.'

'And you won't go to the police?'

'And Kenny Pearce,' added Norman. 'We want to speak to him, too.'

'Kenny's doing installations in the Birmingham area. He won't be back until tomorrow, but he's staying in the Birmingham Travelodge. You'll find him there tonight.

Slater nodded. 'Okay, and what about Crothers?'

'Jason lives in a village called Mossworthy. It's up North, near Durham.'

'Can you write the address down?'

'I don't know the address, just the name of the village.'

'How do we know you're telling the truth?' asked Norman.

'How do I know you won't go to the police?'

'We won't go to the police because we don't have to,' said Slater, getting to his feet. 'They're already looking into your company. I would expect a visit anytime soon.'

'You bastard!'

Slater smiled down at him. 'Yeah, sorry about that. It just goes to show you can't trust anyone these days.'

'We'll be off now, Malcolm,' said Norman, cheerfully. 'Take care.'

'D'YOU and Jane have anything planned for tonight?' Slater asked Norman as they climbed into the car.

'Nothing special,' said Norman. 'So if you're suggesting we should head straight on up to Birmingham, I think we should go for it.'

'Do you want to give her a call and let her know you won't be back until late?'

'No. She'll be fine. It's good to have some time apart, you know?'

Slater looked at Norman, but his partner stared resolutely forward and didn't even glance across at him.

'You make it sound like your relationship is hard work,' observed Slater.

'We just like to give each other a bit of space now and then,' said Norman.

'Is everything okay between you two?'

'Why wouldn't it be?' snapped Norman.

'Easy Tiger,' said Slater. 'There's no need to bite my head off. I'm just looking out for you, that's all.'

He glanced across at Norman, but there was no eye contact i return.

Norman heaved a sigh.

'Jane and I are fine,' he said. 'Just because we don't spend minute together like you and Stella doesn't mean there's a pro you ever have a relationship that lasts more than five minu understand what I mean.'

Slater felt that remark had been uncalled for, and for a split second he had a sharp retort on the tip of his tongue, but with an effort, he managed to keep it inside. Something was obviously bothering Norman, but whatever it was, allowing himself to be drawn into an argument about it was unlikely to help.

'Birmingham it is, then,' he said, finally.

'Right,' said Norman.

'Can you find an address for this hotel and load it into the Satnav?' asked Slater.

Norman fished his phone from his pocket and started searching.

31

At 6 pm they were parked in the Birmingham Travelodge car park. Slater was sitting in the car waiting, while Norman had gone inside to check if Kenny Pearce was in the hotel. Now Norman appeared, heading back to the car carrying two coffees.

'The receptionist says he's not back yet,' he said, climbing back into the car.

Slater took the coffee Norman offered him and looked around the hotel car park.

'Well, if he's driving one of Keeling Security's vans, he'll be easy enough to spot.'

Over the next half hour, the light began to fade. Several cars came into the car park, but there was no sign of Kenny Pearce.

'Of course, Keeling could have sent us up here just to get us out of the way,' said Norman.

'Yeah, he could be playing for time,' said Slater, 'but my hunch is he's willing to sacrifice Pearce and deny any involvement if Pearce starts making accusations.'

'That won't wash,' said Norman. 'The fact he's taken the guy on with a criminal record points the finger at him straight away.'

'You think he'll take Crothers down with him?'

'I'm sure of it,' said Norman. 'He'll be singing at the top of his voice if he thinks it'll save his own neck.'

A pair of headlights came into view as a vehicle pulled into the car park.

'Here we go,' said Slater. 'It's a white van.'

'That must be him,' said Norman. 'Look, it's got the Keeling logo on the side.'

They watched as the driver eased the van into a parking space. He switched his engine off but stayed in his seat.

'What's he doing?' asked Norman.

'I can't see. Maybe he's doing paperwork?'

'No, it's not that. He's just sitting there looking around the car park.'

'He's looking at the car park entrance,' said Slater. 'He's expecting someone to arrive!'

'This could be interesting,' said Norman.

Just then another set of headlights appeared, and another vehicle rolled slowly into the car park. The car paused just inside the car park entrance as if the driver was looking for something or someone. After about twenty seconds the vehicle moved forward and now they could make out what it was.

Norman let out a low whistle.

'Well, well, look at that,' he said. 'A 4x4 Merc. Are you thinking what I'm thinking?'

'Jason Crothers?'

'It's got to be, hasn't it?'

'Let's see what happens. If it is Crothers maybe he'll even have Mickey with him.'

'If we play this right we could get a lot of questions answered here.'

The Mercedes pulled up alongside the van so the two drivers could speak through their open windows. The driver kept his engine running.

'It doesn't look like they're going to go inside,' said Slater.

'Keeping that engine running suggests he doesn't intend to hang around,' said Norman. 'Maybe I should slip out of the car and try to listen in.'

'It's worth a try,' said Slater.

Norman eased his door open, slipped from his seat, and quietly pushed the door closed. Casually he walked across the car park towards the hotel, but as soon as he cleared Slater's car, the Mercedes driver hit the gas and was away. The vehicle had cleared the car park before either of them had time to react. As he watched the tail lights disappearing, Slater slapped his steering wheel in frustration.

'Shit!'

Meanwhile, showing a surprising turn of speed, Norman had managed to run across to the van, reach inside the window and grab the ignition keys.

'Here, piss off mate,' shouted the driver. 'What the bloody hell do you think you're doing?'

'I'm just making sure you can't do a runner like your mate, Jason,' said Norman.

'Who?'

'Jason Crothers. The guy you were just talking to.'

'I dunno—'

'Don't give us that crap,' said Slater as he pulled open the passenger door and climbed in next to Pearce. 'We know who Crothers is, we know who you are, and we know all about your little scam to find new clients.'

Pearce looked at Slater, and then back at Norman. His eyes widened, and he licked his lips.

'You can't do—'

'Sure we can,' said Slater. He reached up and switched on the interior light. 'That's better. Now we can all see what we're doing.'

'Move over,' said Norman, opening the driver's door. 'There's room for three on that bench seat, and you're gonna be the piggy in the middle.'

Norman climbed in next to Pearce, forcing him into the middle seat. Slater produced a pair of handcuffs, snapped them around

Pearce's left wrist, and then around the tee bar automatic gear shift. There was no way Pearce would be able to escape without a key.

'What is this?' asked Pearce. 'A hijacking?'

Norman laughed.

'Now that would be ironic, wouldn't it?'

'I bet there's some really hot stuff in the back of this van,' said Slater. 'Isn't that right, Kenny? How many houses have you broken into this week?'

'I dunno what you mean. I install security systems.'

'Yeah, sure you do, but first of all, you break into them, just to prove to the owners that they need security. Then when you fit the system, you make a note of all the settings so you can come back at a later date, disable the system and rob them all over again.'

'Nice work if you can get it, right?' said Norman. 'And, of course, with your pal Jason providing all the leads you get it rather a lot.'

'Who are you blokes?' cried Pearce. 'Are you the police?'

'No, we're not the police,' said Slater, 'but they'll be along before too long. They're going to take Keeling Security apart, and when they do they'll be putting you and Jason, and Malcolm, away for a long time.'

Pearce licked his lips again.

'So you're looking to make some sort of deal, right?' he asked.

'Anything's possible,' said Norman.

'What's in it for me? Do I get to make a run for it before they get here?'

'That depends on how helpful you are.'

'Okay, So what do you want?'

'You gave Jason Crothers an alibi two years ago,' said Slater.

'You'll have to be a bit more specific if you want me to remember.'

'This was a regular thing, then?'

'I was always covering for him, so his wife didn't find out what he was up to.'

'So you knew what he was doing?'

'I knew he was screwing around, yeah. He seemed to have a way with women. He always had at least one bit on the side.'

'You sound as if you envied him,' said Slater.

Pearce grinned, conspiratorially.

'Yeah, well, we'd all like a bit more action in our lives, wouldn't we?'

'You're sure about that, are you?' asked Slater.

'What does that mean?' demanded Pearce.

'We'll come back to that in a minute,' said Norman. 'But first I want you to recall one specific alibi.'

'Go on then, give us a clue.'

'About two years ago, Jason's sports car got smashed up.'

'I remember. Some kid nicked it and smashed it up, didn't they? He was in a right state over it. I couldn't see what the big deal was. After all, it was just a car, and it was insured.'

'Why did you give him an alibi for that night?'

'Because he asked me. He said he was with some married bird, and if his wife found out she'd go mad.'

'So you lied for him?'

'Sure, why not? If I had a wife like his, I'd be cheating, too,' said Pearce. 'I suppose you win some and you lose some. He definitely lost out there.'

'So you know where he was?'

'Well, no, not exactly. I told everyone Jason was with me playing snooker, but I couldn't tell you exactly where he was.'

'You were both staying at a hotel in Norfolk, is that right?'

'We were there for a few nights.'

'How long was Jason gone on the night his car got trashed?'

'Gawd, I dunno. It was two years ago!'

'Think, Kenny. This is important.'

'It was a Saturday. I know I saw him at breakfast, but I didn't see him again until some time on Sunday.'

'So he would have had time to drive down to Hampshire and back again?'

'I know he looked like he hadn't slept all night, but I don't think it was because he'd been driving.' He winked at Slater. 'Know what I mean? Nudge, nudge, wink, wink. Lucky sod...'

'Lucky sod? So you were jealous of him?'

'Not jealous, just envious. I never had much luck with women myself.'

'You like women, then?' said Slater. 'Not young girls?'

Pearce looked deeply offended.

'What's that supposed to mean?' he said, clenching his fists. 'Are you suggesting I'm some sort of weirdo?'

'Calm down, Kenny, calm down,' said Norman. 'We know you're a thief. We have no reason to think you're a nonce.'

'Why say it, then?'

Norman ignored the question.

'The girl who is supposed to have stolen the car was fourteen, did you know that?' he asked. 'And you say Jason was in a state about the car?'

'Yeah, that's right.' They could almost hear the whirring and clicking inside Kenny Pearce's head as he began to make sense of what they were saying. 'Hang on a minute. Are you saying... You mean you think he was... with young girls...'

'Let me spell it out, so you're in no doubt,' said Slater. 'We believe Jason Crothers was having an affair with the fourteen-year-old girl who died in the crash that night. We also believe he was with her at the time of the crash, and that he was driving.'

'No, no, no. That can't be right. Jason likes them married. I've seen some of them...'

'Yes, he does like them married, but only if they have daughters aged around twelve to fourteen,' said Slater.

'It looks like you're in even deeper shit than we thought,' said Norman, cheerfully. 'Not only are you going to go to prison for breaking and entering, but you'll also be in there for conspiring to enable a sex offender—'

'Now wait a minute, you've got that wrong. He's not like that. Even if he is, I didn't know—'

'Yeah, tell that to the judge,' said Slater.

Norman produced a set of handcuffs and snapped them around Pearce's right wrist.

'Here, what are you doing? You can't—'

'I just did,' said Norman, 'and it's quite possible my next move is going to be snapping the cuffs onto the steering wheel and leaving you here for the police to clean up.'

'But you said we had a deal!'

'I said it was possible, but then I didn't know you were assisting Crothers with his dirty little habit.'

'But I wasn't. Well, not on purpose. What about making another deal? Is that possible?'

'Well, as I said, anything's possible. Maybe you can help us, and help yourself at the same time. Understand?'

Pearce's face lit up as he saw a glimmer of hope.

'What d'you wanna know?

'Jason Crothers? Where does he live?'

Pearce's face fell.

'Shit! I dunno. I know he used to live in a village called East Winton, but he's moved a couple of times since his wife kicked him out. I dunno exactly where he lives now. He never told me.'

Norman snapped the handcuffs onto the steering wheel.

'As you said, Kenny, you win some, and you lose some.'

'You can't do this,' screamed Pearce.

'Kenny, you have to stop saying we can't do stuff we've already done. It's like insisting black is white. It's ridiculous,' said Norman. He looked across at Slater. 'Are you ready to go?'

'Yeah, I guess so.'

'No,' begged Pearce. 'Don't leave me here like this. I'll die!'

'Don't be absurd,' said Slater. 'You won't die. It's not cold, you're not starving, and you have a bottle of water. The police will be here in a couple of hours. You'll be fine.'

'The police? You haven't called the police, have you?'

'As soon as I get back in my car, I'll call my local force,' said Slater. 'Of course, they'll have to call the police up here, and then they'll come and pick you up. It'll take a lot of calls to coordinate it all, and it'll probably take a bit more than a couple of hours, but I'm sure they'll get here eventually.'

He reached up and switched off the interior light. 'It'll give you a little privacy,' he assured Pearce.

They opened the doors together, slipped from their seats, closed the doors and headed back to their car.

'That's it then,' said Norman. 'Jason must have been driving the night Lilly died.'

'It certainly looks that way.'

'So, why don't I feel pleased we worked it out?'

'I know what you mean,' said Slater, gloomily. 'The only glimmer of light in all this is that we can now prove Lilly wasn't a car thief.'

'That doesn't seem much of a consolation.'

'Yeah, you're right about that.'

'Are you gonna call Stella and report all this?'

'I suppose I should.'

'Are you having second thoughts?'

'It's just that—'

'Wait. Are you telling me you're not going to report it?' asked Norman. 'This could be murder we're talking about.'

'The police could have found all this out two years ago if they'd wanted to, but they preferred to believe a young girl stole a car.'

'You think someone went for the easy answer?'

'I think someone couldn't be arsed to turn a few stones over and see what crawled out.'

'So what do you suggest we do?'

'If we hand this over now, we'll almost certainly be totally excluded from the rest of the inquiry which means we've done all the work, and they'll get all the credit. I'm not sure I can swallow that.'

'Are you sure about this?' asked Norman.

'What d'you mean?'

'I mean, is it worth falling out with Stella just so you can massage your ego by proving you're better than the police?'

Slater felt his cheeks redden.

'Is that what you think?'

'You have to admit you grab every opportunity to get one over them.'

'No, I don't!'

'Yes, you do, Dave. Every chance you get. You know it, and I know it.'

'But if they did their job properly...'

'Are you saying they're all bent?'

'Of course not.'

'Okay, so are you telling me you've never made a mistake?'

'Well, yeah, sure, I've made plenty.'

'And yet you expect everyone else to be perfect.'

'That's not what I'm saying.'

'Sure it is,' said Norman. 'You seem to have forgotten what it's like for them. Wasn't it the never-ending cuts, and the relentless pressure to produce results, that finally made you quit?'

'Yeah, bu—'

'Don't you think it's the same for everyone else?'

'I suppose so, ye—'

'So can you really blame someone for grabbing the chance for a quick result? Based on the evidence before them, it was an open and shut case. Why dig deeper when there was no need?'

Slater felt trapped. Deep down he knew there was truth in what Norman was saying, so why did he find it so hard to admit?

'I suppose when you put it like that...' he said. 'I didn't realise I was that bad.'

'I wouldn't beat yourself up about it,' said Norman. 'I just think sometimes you're too quick to put them down. You need to remember none of us is perfect.'

'Yeah, thanks. I think I've got the message.'

Norman looked at Slater.

'You're not going to sulk on the way home now, are you?'

Slater sighed.

'I guess I don't like to hear uncomfortable truths about myself, but I know you're right, so no, I'm not going to sulk on the way home.'

'I can't tell you how pleased I am to hear you say that,' said Norman. 'But you still have to decide what you're going to do about Stella.'

'I thought you made it quite clear what I should do.'

'All I said was you need to be careful you don't let this come between you.'

'Now I'm confused,' said Slater. 'Didn't you say I should pass the case over?'

'Actually, no I didn't. I just pointed out how you seem to feel it's a competition all the time.'

'What does that mean?'

'I don't like the idea of them taking the credit for our work, and then shutting us out, any more than you do,' said Norman, 'but I don't think it's worth you falling out with Stella. D'you?'

'I need to speak with her,' said Slater. 'But are you sure you're okay about that?'

'Absolutely. A good relationship is worth more than a bit of dented pride.'

32

'So, what did Stella say when you told her?' asked Norman next morning.

'I think the fact she's leaving has worked in our favour,' said Slater.

'She's really gonna leave?'

'She feels she has no choice. Having spent the last few months behind a desk, she knows she doesn't want to carry on doing that.'

'I can understand that,' said Norman, 'but it's a pity she has to give up. I know how hard it was for me. What's she going to do?'

'She hasn't decided yet. I think she plans on taking some time out to think about her future.'

'Good for her. There's no point in rushing a decision like that. So, how has this worked in our favour?'

'We struck a deal,' said Slater. 'She's going to pass on what we know about Keeling Security, but give us 48 hours before she does anything else.'

'She's taking a risk this close to her leaving date. She could get kicked out with nothing if they find out sh—'

'We only have 48 hours as long as she doesn't find anything while they're poking around at Keeling Security. As far as anyone else is concerned, I only told her about Keeling and Crothers and their scam.

'After 48 hours she will pass on the information about Jason Crothers as well. But, if anything comes up in the meantime that even suggests what else Crothers was up to, she won't be able to stop whatever happens after that.'

'So, we're in a race, and we have a possible 48 hour start?'

'That's about the size of it.'

'And all we know is that the guy we're looking for lives in a village, that's at the other end of the country.'

'I was thinking about that,' said Slater. 'How do we know Malcolm Keeling wasn't lying about that?'

'We don't. So, what do we do?'

'I think we need to ask a few more questions before we go charging up North.'

'What questions?' asked Norman.

'I don't know about you, but I find it hard to believe Mia Crothers doesn't know where Jason lives.'

'Yeah, I have to admit it seems unlikely.'

'He funds her lifestyle, Norm. She's got nothing without him. She must know where he is.'

'You want to go and lean on her, right? I think that's a great idea, but what are you going to use as leverage?'

'Remember when Tim told us about his connection with Jason Crothers? He said Crothers had an affair with his wife.'

'That's right,' agreed Norman, 'and then she committed suicide because of it.'

'Ah, yes, but did she?' asked Slater. 'It was his daughter, Jeanie, who took her own life first.'

Norman looked perplexed. 'I'm afraid you'll have to fill the blanks in for me,' he said.

'Tim told us he lost everything because of what Jason Crothers had done, right?' explained Slater. 'Now, at the time we both assumed he meant the affair, but what if he meant something else? What if Crothers had targeted young Jeanie? Tim's wife had moved in with the guy and took her daughter with her. Then a week later Crothers left.'

'Now I see where you're going with this,' said Norman. 'So you think Jeanie committed suicide because Crothers had attacked her, and then Tim's wife blamed herself because, in effect, she had enabled the monster to commit the crime.'

'Exactly!' said Slater. 'She blamed herself, couldn't live with it, and took an overdose to end it all.'

'Holy crap!' said Norman. 'So you think Tim knows what Crothers is really like.'

Slater shrugged his shoulders.

'It adds up, doesn't it?' he said.

'But if he saw Crothers by the car that night,' asked Norman, 'and then learned how old Lilly was, why didn't he come forward and tell the police?'

'Because he wants his own justice. An eye for an eye, isn't that what he said?'

'But he knows Crothers doesn't live around here anymore, and he's known it for ages, so why is he still here?'

'Mia?'

'He said he wasn't intending to hurt her and that it's Crothers he wants to kill.'

'D'you believe that? Don't forget when we suggested revenge was a crazy idea he said he had every right to be insane.'

'I think we need to speak to him again, urgently,' said Norman.

'Let's go and see Mia Crothers first, just to make sure she's safe,' said Slater.

33

A gardener was weeding not far from the front door of Mia Crothers' house when Slater and Norman pulled up. He nodded to them but continued with his work as they walked up to the front door and Norman reached for the bell.

'You've got some nerve, turning up here again,' she sneered, when she opened the door. 'I don't know how you have the gall to—'

'Before you get carried away insulting us,' said Norman, 'you should be aware we know about your husband and his hobby.'

'Keeping vintage sports cars isn't a crime, is it?'

'No,' said Norman, 'but that wasn't what I was talking about, and I think you know exactly what I mean.'

'I don't think I do.'

Norman looked pointedly at the nearby gardener.

'D'you really want to do this out here, Mrs Crothers?'

Mia glanced at the gardener, and licked her lips.

'You'd better come in,' she said.

She let them into the hall, then closed the door.

'How dare you come here making accusations—'

'Are you denying your husband was grooming young girls for sex,' said Slater.

'Young girls? I don't know anything about that. I know he's a womaniser, but young girls? I don't think so.'

'All three of us know that's not true, Mia,' said Norman. 'At first we couldn't figure out why you hated Lilly so much over a crashed car. Sure, anyone would have been annoyed at having a car written off, but in the end it was just a car. Most people would get over it, but you didn't, and we couldn't see why that was. It wasn't even your car, was it?'

Mia's lips had narrowed so much they almost disappeared, but she said nothing.

'Lilly was a friend of the family and yet you didn't have an ounce of sympathy for her, or for her mother,' continued Norman. 'Then we found out about Jason, and we realised— you weren't upset about the car, were you? You were upset that your husband had been having an affair with a fourteen-year-old.'

'That's not true!'

'I don't know if you realise it, Mrs Crothers,' said Slater, 'but having sex with a minor is statutory rape.'

Her mouth flapped uselessly once or twice.

'No-one raped that girl. She knew what she was doing. She was nothing but a cheap little tart.'

'She was under sixteen,' said Slater. 'Whichever way you want to dress it up, she was too young to consent.'

'My husband never had sex with that girl.'

'I think you're in denial, Mia,' said Norman.

'What about Jeanie Sellars?' asked Slater.

Mia's eyes widened.

'Who?'

'Jeanie Sellars.'

'I don't think I know that name.'

'Sure you do,' said Slater. 'She took her own life, not long before you and Jason moved down here.'

Mia swallowed hard, but didn't say anything.

'Jason lured her mother into sharing a flat with him,' said Slater, 'but it was Jeanie he was really interested in. A week later Jason fled, probably because Jeanie's mother had realised what he was up to. She probably realised too late, though, because within a few days Jeanie had committed suicide. Her mother blamed herself and took her own life a couple of days later.'

'When was this,' her voice was barely more than a whisper.

'About five years ago,' said Norman. 'When you lived in Harrogate.'

'Harrogate?' she whispered, her hand rising to cover her mouth.

'All adding up now, is it?' asked Slater.

'That tramp you told me about,' said Norman. 'The one who was looking for Jason? His name's Harvey Sellars. He's Jeanie's father. He wants to find Jason because he wants to avenge his wife and daughter.'

'This isn't true,' she said. 'It's true we moved South because there was a scandal after the suicides, but we were hoping to do it anyway because it suited Jason better for work.'

Norman looked at Slater. It was obvious Slater felt she had known about Jeanie all along.

'We need to know what Harvey said to you and what you told him,' said Norman.

'All he said was that he was looking for Jason, and that he was an old school friend.'

'And you didn't recognise him?'

'Why would I? I knew of him, but I had never actually met him before. If he had told me his name I probably would have made the connection, but he didn't.'

'I should tell you we know of at least two other under-age girls Jason has been grooming,' said Norman.

'Are you still suggesting you know nothing about it?' asked Slater.

'It's just not true. Mickey must never know about any of these allegations,' she demanded.

'I'm afraid he may already know,' said Norman.

Her eyes nearly popped out of her head.

'What do you mean?'

'Mickey knows Harvey Sellars.'

'That's not possible. How could he?'

'Was Mickey here when Harvey called?' asked Norman.

'No.'

'Are you sure?'

'I suppose he could have been.'

'Maybe he overheard the conversation.'

'But even so, I can't believe he would befriend a man like that?

'It's true,' said Slater. 'He even created a website for Harvey and set up a site for people to make donations. Mickey thinks Harvey is a hero!'

'But this can't be true. Mickey's a good boy. He would have told me.'

'Mia, we don't know for sure, but Mickey may be in danger,' said Norman. 'Harvey lost his wife and daughter, and he told us he wants an eye for an eye. We know he wants to find Jason, but—'

'You think he's going to kill Mickey?' she shrieked.

'We think it's unlikely. We believe Jason is the only target, but we can't be sure.'

'Then we have to find him.'

'So give us Jason's address,' said Slater.

'I don't know—'

'That's bullshit,' snapped Slater. 'You know exactly where he lives. What are you going to do if Harvey gets there before us, and he turns on Mickey, too?'

She looked shocked, as if Slater had just slapped her, but his words had the desired effect.

'Yes, you're right. We need to go there. He lives in a village called Mossworthy, not far from Oxford.'

'Malcolm Keeling told us Mossworthy was near Durham,' said Norman.

'I know where my own husband lives!'

'We need to get up there,' said Slater.

'Let me come with you,' she begged. 'This is my son we're talking about.'

Slater wasn't keen, but when he looked at Norman he could see his partner didn't feel the same way.

'It might be a good idea,' said Norman. 'We don't know what we're going to find up there and at least we'll know she's safe from Harvey.'

'Speaking of Harvey, we need to find him before we go,' said Slater.

'Mia,' said Norman. 'We need to speak to Harvey before we go, but I don't think it's a good idea for you to come with us. Will you wait here until we come back?'

'You promise you'll come back for me?'

'Of course.'

34

As Slater drove into the lay-by that morning, Tim was standing by the driver's side of the old car. He had something in his hand, but they couldn't make out exactly what it was. When he saw them, he put whatever it was into his pocket and walked the short distance to his regular seat before the old brazier.

'Oh there you are,' said Tim, when they reached him. 'When you said you were going to be coming back I didn't think it would take so long. I was expecting you yesterday.'

'Sorry if we disappointed you,' said Slater, 'but I don't recall saying when we'd be back.'

'No,' agreed Tim, 'but I thought you'd be clever enough to have worked it all out a bit quicker that's all.'

'Worked out what?'

Tim smiled and shook his head.

'Nice try,' said Tim, 'but I'm not that daft.' He studied Slater's face for a moment. 'Oh wait! You haven't worked it out, have you?'

'Seeing as you're so clever, and we're obviously so dim, why don't you tell us?' suggested Norman.

Tim looked up at the sky. He seemed to be working something out in his head, but it was only for a second or two.

'I tell you what,' he said. 'As you've got this far, I'll fill you in on the rest. It's too late for you to stop it now anyway.'

'Stop what?'

'I'll get to that.' Tim pointed to two upturned buckets. 'Why don't you pull up a seat.'

They settled around the old brazier.

'I told you why I came here, didn't I?' Tim began.

'To kill Jason Crothers, yeah, we know that,' said Slater, irritably. 'What we can't figure out is why you're still here when you know he lives a good fifty miles North of here.'

'Unless you intend to kill Mia Crothers first,' suggested Norman.

'Mia? Oh, no, I don't intend to kill her. I never even intended for her to bang her head that day. I was quite upset about that.'

'So why are you still here?'

'Alibi. I can't be in Oxford and down here, now can I?'

'Why d'you need an alibi?'

'For when Jason dies, of course.' He studied their faces. 'You really haven't worked it out, have you?'

Norman sighed.

'Okay, look, you're obviously thinking way above our level, and we're never going to work out this amazing plan of yours, so why don't you stop messing around and just tell us?'

Tim smiled indulgently.

'Jason Crothers is a pervert who was responsible for the death of my daughter, and my wife. I think it's only right that someone like him shouldn't be allowed to get away with that, but I also don't think being put in prison is proper punishment. As I told you before, it should be an eye for an eye.'

'Which is why we thought Mia was in danger,' said Norman.

'Oh no, Mia's not going to die. She's always known what he's like, but as long as the money kept rolling in, she turned a blind eye. Now, in my book, that makes her as bad as him, but she's not going to die; that would be far too good for her. I've got a special punishment for her.'

What's that?'

'You'll see, you'll see.'

'You're beginning to sound like a mad man,' said Slater.

'You're probably right,' said Tim, his smile rapidly disappearing, 'but I did tell you I had good reason to be insane, didn't I? The thing is I wasn't joking.'

He seemed to have lost his thread for a moment.

'Where was I?' he muttered. 'Oh yes, the plan. I didn't really know what I was going to do when I first got to this village. Even when I discovered where Crothers lived I wasn't sure, but slowly, and surely, I developed a plan. So, it's been a long time in the planning, but I think it's been worth it in the end.'

'Unless you tell us what this grand plan is, we're going to have to take your word for that,' said Slater, unhappily.

Tim glared at him.

'You need to get rid of that chip on your shoulder,' he advised. 'It'll wear you down if you're not careful.'

Norman fully expected Slater to go off on one at this point, but to his surprise, his colleague kept a straight face and didn't rise to the bait.

'The plan,' encouraged Norman.

'Oh yes,' said Tim. 'You see, I didn't know where Crothers lived until after the accident. But when I saw the story about the crash in the newspaper, I knew the man I had seen at the scene must be him. It was easy to find out where he lived after that.

'Once the heat had died down, I went to the house, but Mia told me he was gone. Of course, I didn't believe her at first, so I staked out their house, but they never showed, and I thought I'd lost my chance. However, completely by chance, I struck gold because the boy, Mickey, must have seen me talking to his mother, and he came to find me. Of course, once we got talking, it was quite easy to reel him in. Crothers groomed my daughter for sex so, as part of my revenge, I groomed his son for murder. It's poetic justice, don't you think?'

Norman's phone beeped.

'D'you want to get that?' asked Tim.

'It's just a text message. It can wait. You still didn't tell us about this special punishment for Mia Crothers.'

'She's going to watch her precious little boy get put away for murdering his father.'

Norman's mouth popped open.

'Why would he murder his father?' asked Slater.

'Jealousy is a compelling motivation, even in one so young. As I said, I've been grooming him for a long time. The thing is, he wanted Lilly all for himself. Finding out his father had got in there before him, well, that would make anyone jealous, wouldn't it?'

'So that's the real reason you gave him Lilly's phone,' said Slater.

'Exhibit A, as you might say,' said Tim. 'Lot's of evidence on there. Old messages, photos, you name it, she saved it. But the most important thing was a contact called "J".'

'You think "J" was Jason Crothers?'

'I don't think it's him, I know it is. He was "J" to my wife, and to my daughter. It's got to be him.'

'And you've told Mickey all this?' asked Slater.

Tim smiled but said nothing.

'So that's why he suddenly wanted to see his father,' said Norman.

'It's a great plan, don't you agree?' said Tim.

'You're sick,' said Slater.

'As I said, that would be my defence, but I don't think I'll need it, do you?'

Norman was checking his phone.

'Vinnie says Mickey switched his phone on about ten minutes ago and received a text message,' he told Slater. 'It was sent from here.'

'Have you got a mobile phone in your pocket?' Slater asked Tim.

Tim smiled.

'Oh my, you're terrific aren't you,' he said, pointing to the brazier, 'but I'm afraid you're a little late. I put it in there when I saw your car.'

'What was in that text?' demanded Norman.

'Now shall I tell you, or shan't I?' said Tim, thoughtfully.

Slater took a step towards him, but he didn't flinch, merely holding his hand up, palm facing outwards.

'Ah, so that's it, is it? If I don't tell you, you think you can beat it out of me.'

Slater was suitably embarrassed.

'If you'd just stop pissing around and tell us what the hell you're playing at...'

'You feel impotent don't you?' asked Tim. 'It's frustrating, isn't it? Believe me, I know. I spent years like that, but in the long run, being made to wait so long to get my revenge has enabled me to come up with such an ingenious plan, it's made this whole experience much more worthwhile.'

'Dave's right. You're not right in the head, are you?' suggested Norman.

'I repeat, it's a great defence, in the unlikely event I should need one,' said Tim.

'You won't get away with this,' said Slater.

'Of course, I will. It's probably happening right now as we speak. Best of all, as you said yourself, I'm fifty miles from the scene. I even have two detectives who can give me an alibi.'

Norman jumped to his feet.

'Come on, Dave. Let's get out of here. This is a total waste of time. This guy's full of shit.'

'The text message I sent,' said Tim, 'had the pin number for the phone I gave Mickey. He was already primed by what I told him, but now he will have seen the evidence for himself, and it will prove what I told him is true. It's bye, bye, daddy, time.'

'Come on, Dave,' said Norman. 'We need to get up there before that kid does something that'll ruin his life.'

'You'll be too late,' taunted Tim.

'Yeah, well, we'll see about that,' said Slater, running for his car.

TWENTY MINUTES later they were heading north towards Oxford, a confused and agitated Mia Crothers strapped into the back seat. Slater had insisted on the way over to collect Mia that, as she loathed him, it would be best if he kept quiet and focused on driving. Norman had agreed with Slater's assessment and reluctantly accepted that it meant he had the task of explaining what they had just heard from Tim to Mia.

'Something's happened, hasn't it?' she had insisted, as soon as she saw their faces. 'I can tell, you know.'

'It seems we were thinking along the right lines, but we weren't exactly spot on,' said Norman, vaguely.

'Norman, I may be a lot of things, but I am not an idiot, and I would appreciate it if you didn't treat me like one,' she said, patiently.

Norman sighed wearily and wondered how exactly should he go about telling her he thought her son was about to kill her ex-husband.

'Let me remind you this is my son we're talking about,' she said. 'Now, will you please tell me what's going on?'

There was a noticeable tremor in her voice. Slater had been reluctant to take her along, and now he wondered how much it would take before she blew a fuse and became a liability. But she was here now so, whatever happened, they would just have to deal with it.

'Okay,' said Norman, 'so, the long and short of it is this; Harvey Sellars, the tramp who came to your house, has been grooming your son.'

'Grooming him? How do you mean "grooming" him?'

'Harvey was there the night Jason's car crashed with Lilly Becker inside. He says Lilly wasn't driving, she was the passenger. The driver survived the crash and moved Lilly's body, so it looked as if she had been driving.'

'I don't see what this has to do with Mickey. He was with me.'

'According to Harvey Sellars, it was your husband, Jason, who was driving, and he's told Mickey about it. He's also given Mickey Lilly's mobile phone which he says proves Lilly and Jason were having an affair.'

'But that's not true,' she said.

'Harvey has convinced Mickey it is true,' said Norman. 'He's told Mickey that his father likes young teenage girls and that Lilly isn't the first. That's why Mickey suddenly decided he wanted to see his father. He's gone there looking to avenge Lilly by killing Jason.'

'He wouldn't do that. He's a good boy—'

'Who tells you everything, yeah, you told us that,' said Norman. 'So how come he didn't tell you about knowing Harvey? And why didn't he tell you he thought his father had been responsible for Lilly's death?'

There was a long silence. It was Slater who broke it.

'Why did you say it's not true when Norm said about Jason driving the car that night?' he asked.

'Because I know it's not true. I know exactly where Jason was that night, and I can assure you he wasn't anywhere near East Winton.'

'If you're talking about him playing snooker all night in a Norfolk hotel, that's all lies,' said Slater.

'Don't you think I know that?'

'So, where was he?'

'I'd rather not say.'

Slater let out a heavy sigh of frustration.

'Mia,' said Norman. 'Your son is about to kill your husband. Don't you think it might change the situation if we can get to him first and prove Jason wasn't driving?'

Now it was her turn to sigh.

'If you must know, he was with his mistress, and I can promise you she's not a teenager.'

'But we have evidence that says he likes teenagers,' said Norman. 'Isn't that why you kicked him out?'

'Jason flatters and flirts with everyone, but he knows when to stop.'

'So why did you kick him out?'

'If you must know, we split up because Jason was having an affair with my sister,' she hissed. 'He has a roving eye, and he is a womaniser, but he is not a pervert.'

'But what about Harrogate? When we spoke about it before, you said—'

'That was an accusation Harvey Sellars made, but the police

investigated and didn't find any evidence. Nothing was ever proved. I believe it was an accusation made out of a desire for revenge. I understand the motivation behind it, but that doesn't make it right.

'I've never had reason to think Jason liked young girls, and if I ever had, I would have reported him to the police myself.'

Slater exchanged a glance with Norman who looked just as confused as he, himself, was feeling. Although he couldn't see Mia's face, she certainly sounded as if she was telling the truth, but could they really have got it so wrong? Or, was she just in denial?

'I understand you don't want to believe Jason could have been into young girls,' he said, 'but we have two other mothers who claim he was trying it on with their daughters.'

'And there's a wife here who claims they've got it wrong,' she said.

'I admire your loyalty,' said Norman. 'A lot of wives in your position would be only too happy to hang their husband out to dry.'

'Don't get me wrong,' she said. 'I hope he rots in hell for what he's done to me, but I won't accuse him of something I know isn't true.'

'So, you don't think the "J' in Lilly Becker's phone is Jason?' asked Slater.

'What's the number?' she asked. 'I can soon tell you if it's his.'

Slater and Norman exchanged a guilty look.

'Er, we haven't actually seen the number,' admitted Norman.

She snorted in derision.

'Huh! So you don't even know if what he's told you is true. Isn't that called hearsay? I thought you two were supposed to be real detectives, but you're no better than Harvey Sellars, are you? You're accusing Jason of all sorts here yet you don't seem to have a shred of real evidence!'

They travelled on in stony silence, each lost in their own thoughts until eventually, Mia spoke again.

'How much longer is this going to take?'

'About ten minutes,' said Slater.

35

The house in Mossworthy was a small, unassuming, detached cottage. As they pulled up on the road outside, Slater couldn't help thinking it looked an unlikely setting for the drama that was quite possibly about to unfold. They climbed from the car and marched up the short drive to the house. As they approached, the front door opened to reveal a familiar figure.

'Oh, God what's she doing here?' hissed Mia.

Norman looked at Slater.

'Isn't that Diana Williams from Keeling Security?' he asked.

'So, you've met my sister?' asked Mia. 'Oh well, at least I won't have to make any introductions.'

'Thank goodness you're here,' said Diana as they reached the front door. Her face was etched with concern. 'Mickey has Jason trapped in the kitchen, and he has a knife!'

'Oh crap!' said Norman, pushing his way past her. 'That's not good.'

'Is there a back door?' Slater asked Diana, as Norman and Mia rushed towards the kitchen.

She pointed around the side of the house. 'Round that way.'

Slater ran down the side of the house, Diana following. He slowed to a stop as he reached the back corner, and turned to Diana.

'You'd better stay back,' he said, quietly. 'Okay?'

She nodded her head.

Slater eased his way along the back wall, keeping his back against it until he could peer into the window. It was a big, square kitchen with a massive pine table in the centre. Mickey was this side, with his back to the window. He seemed to be pointing a knife at Jason, who was on the opposite side of the table. Jason appeared to be trying to reason with his son, but Slater couldn't hear what they were saying.

He crouched down until he was low enough to creep, unseen, across to the other side of the window where there was a back door which appeared to lead straight into the kitchen. Carefully he crept across to the door, raised himself to his full height and peered through the window in the door. Mickey still had his back to the door, but precisely what he was going to do now he was here, Slater didn't know. But he was sure he would think of something. He just needed Norm and Mia to create some sort of diversion.

Meanwhile, as Slater watched and wondered, on the other side of the kitchen Norman and Mia had now reached the door.

Mia looked at Norman for guidance. He nodded his head.

'Go ahead and speak to him. He'll know your voice.'

'Mickey?' she called, through the door. 'Darling, it's Mummy. I know you're upset about Lilly, but I promise you it wasn't Daddy's fault.'

Norman couldn't help feel the names "Mummy" and "Daddy" were somewhat incongruous in this potentially deadly situation, but if it was going to give them some thinking time who was he to complain?

'Mum? What are you doing here? I didn't think you even knew where I was?'

'I've told you before,' she said, matter-of-factly. 'I'm your mother. I know everything.'

Norman was both surprised, and impressed, by her coolness. Outside the back door, Slater could see Mickey was becoming suitably distracted. He reached for the door handle, and prayed it wasn't stiff, or squeaky...

Back indoors, Mia was speaking again.

'Listen to me, Mickey,' she said. 'I know what you've been told by that man, but he's wrong. Honestly, your father wasn't there that night.'

'He was,' said Mickey. 'I've seen the text messages they sent each other to arrange things.'

'Have you checked the number? I'm sure it wasn't Daddy's phone.'

'Of course, it wasn't his number,' said Mickey. 'He used a different phone, so no-one would know. Tim told me.'

'I'm afraid Tim was lying to you, darling.'

'Why would he lie?'

'Because he wants to hurt Daddy, but he's not brave enough to do it himself.'

'No, that can't be right,' said Mickey, uncertainly. 'Tim's a war hero. He's not frightened of anything.'

'Mickey,' called Norman. 'My name's Norman. I'm a detective. I've been investigating your friend Tim. His real name is Harvey Sellars. He's not a war hero. He's never been in the Army or any other branch of the Services.'

'You're lying!' cried Mickey.

'Why would I lie?' asked Norman.

This time Mickey didn't reply, and Norman wondered what he might be doing.

'Listen to me Mickey,' he said. 'You've been set up. What your mother said is true. Tim has been grooming you to do his dirty work for him, but it's all based on something he believes that isn't true. If you do this, you'll ruin your life, and for what?'

'How do I know you're telling the truth?' asked Mickey.

'What do I have to do to prove it to you?' asked Norman.

'Aunty Diana can tell you where your father was,' added Mia, beginning to sound a little desperate. 'That will prove he wasn't in the car.'

'Is Diana there?' asked Mickey. 'Let me speak to her.'

Norman and Mia looked around for Diana, but she was nowhere to be seen. Then, there was a loud crash from inside the kitchen, followed by the sounds of a scuffle, and a fair amount of cursing. Without a moment's thought, Norman barged his way through the door.

The back door was wide open. Diana Williams was standing in the doorway, hands to her face, staring down at a tangle of bodies on the kitchen floor.

'Jeez,' said Norman, as he ran around the table, Mia hot on his heels. 'What the hell...'

As they reached the other side of the table, Jason stepped back and pulled his son to his feet. Mia immediately enveloped her son in her arms. Slater was still lying on the floor. He was clutching his left hand, and a small pool of blood was forming on the floor. He looked up at Norman.

'Little bugger cut my bloody hand,' he muttered.

Norman bent down and helped him to his feet.

'Did he try to stab you?' he asked.

'No. It was my fault. I shouldn't have tried to grab the knife with my bare hands.'

'You're right, it was your fault,' agreed Norman. 'That certainly wasn't your most sensible move.'

'Well, pardon me for not coming equipped with armour plated gloves,' said Slater, huffily.

'Here,' said Norman. 'You'd better run that hand under the tap while I find something to clean your wound.'

'There's a first aid kit, under the sink,' suggested Diana. 'Here, let me do it.'

While she cleaned Slater's hand and dressed his wound, he asked her a couple of questions.

'Is it true Jason was with you that night?'

'Yes, it is.'

'How long has it been going on?'

'It started a few months before that night, but at that stage, it was a casual relationship. It took a while before we decided we belonged together. We're living together most of the time now. As soon as I sell my house, I'll be living here permanently.'

'Does Mia know?'

'I have no idea. Instead of facing up to the truth, she prefers to shut us out and pretend we don't exist.'

'Ah. I see. What about Mickey? What does he think?'

'I think he's a little confused right now,' she said. 'We wanted to tell him, that's why I'm here. But things took a turn for the worse before we got that far.'

'She tells us he's a womaniser,' said Slater. 'What makes you think he won't start cheating on you?'

'I'm not sure that's actually any of your business,' she said.

Slater smiled. 'Fair enough,' he said.

'But if you must know, I would like to think I'm not my sister. She can be difficult. She's as much to blame as Jason is.'

'There is one thing,' said Slater. 'I thought he would have a bit of an Irish accent, but he doesn't does he?'

She laughed.

'Who, Jason? Irish? Why on earth did you think that?'

'It's just something someone said. I must have got the wrong end of the stick. Can I ask you something else?'

'Go on.'

'What's the thing with him and Malcolm Keeling?'

'How do you mean?'

'Well, Keeling fired him, and now he employs him as a consultant.'

'Malcolm and Jason weren't getting on. I don't know what the problem was, because Jason doesn't talk about it, but the fling with Keira Silver was just an excuse.'

'But whatever it was has blown over now, right?' asked Slater. 'I mean, Jason works as a consultant now, so I guess that means they've made up their differences.'

'I would say it's an uneasy truce,' said Diana. 'There's no love lost between them. I can tell you that much.'

'Why?'

'Now, that I can't tell you.'

'D'you know when they fell out?'

'I first noticed it a couple of years ago.'

Norman had come into the kitchen.

'How's the hero?' he asked.

'It's not a deep cut; I think he'll survive,' said Diana.

'Are we finished here, Dave?' asked Norman. 'Only no-one got hurt, so there's no need to call the police. Besides, I think we need to get back. I have an urgent need to speak to a man who lives in a car.'

'What about Mia, and Mickey?'

'I think Mia, Mickey, and Jason actually plan on speaking to each other.'

'Really?' said Diana.

'I think they'd like you to join them, too,' said Norman.

Diana didn't look sure.

'Honestly,' said Norman. 'They told me to ask you to join them.'

36

Five minutes later they were in the car heading back home.

'I take it you spoke to Jason,' said Slater.

'Yeah. He confirms everything Mia said.'

'Diana does, too,' said Slater.

'So it looks like the only liar is Harvey Sellars.'

'They're all hiding something,' said Slater. 'I get the feeling there's this tiny detail they all know, but they aren't telling us.'

'That would explain all the loose ends.'

'Which ones?'

'Well, for a start, what about Keira Silver's daughter?'

'Mia said Jason likes to flatter and flirt,' said Slater. 'What if that's all it was and Keira decided to make a much bigger deal out of it? Or, maybe she just wanted to ruin the guy's reputation for revenge.'

'Hmm. I dunno if I buy that,' said Norman. 'Are you gonna tell me the same thing applies to that Italian lady, Rosabella Rizzi? You see, I think more than one is too much of a coincidence. And who is "J" if it's not Jason?'

'Did Rosabella actually mention Jason by name when you spoke to her?' asked Slater.

Norman thought for a few seconds.

'Now you've put me on the spot, I can't say if she did or not. What are you getting at?'

'We only know about her because she was calling Summer Duval's message service, right? So, was she calling to leave a message for Jason, or was it a message for Josh Ludlow?'

'But didn't we say Malcolm Keeling was Josh Ludlow?'

'That's right, we did,' said Slater.

'So why would she call him?'

'We know Rosabella had a Keeling Security system installed, and then shortly afterwards she was burgled. Then someone from Keeling went to see her, persuaded her to have an upgrade and gave her a bit more on top in the form of a brief affair.'

'Yeah, Jason went to see her.'

'But did he?' insisted Slater. 'We assumed it was him, but did she actually name him, or was he just, "that man from Keeling Security"?'

'You think Malcolm Keeling went to see her?'

'This wasn't a sales call, was it? This was a complaint that had to be handled discreetly. Who better to do that than the guy who owns the company?'

'Where's all this come from?'

'Summer told us Josh Ludlow had an Irish accent. We now know Jason is very English. Diana told me, Jason fell out with Malcolm Keeling about two years ago, although she doesn't know why.'

'Don't forget Diana is Jason's girlfriend. She could easily be lying,' said Norman.

'I think she's telling the truth. So here's an idea: what if Jason and Keeling were good friends. What if they were good enough friends that Jason even let Keeling borrow his car to impress a girlfriend?'

'Jesus! You think Keeling was the one having an affair with Lilly? So Jason would have known he was driving that night, and you think that's why they fell out?'

'It works, doesn't it? And it tells us who "J" is if it's not Jason.'

'But what sort of a guy is Jason if he knew that, but didn't come forward and say so?'

'My guess is he's a blackmailer, and that's why he's now a consultant who can afford to keep Mia happy, and still buy himself that cottage in Mossworthy.'

'So Harvey Sellars, or Tim, or whatever the hell he wants to call himself, has got it completely wrong. Jason didn't interfere with his daughter, nor did he leave Lilly to die all on her own.'

'I think this one's over our heads,' said Slater.

'For sure,' said Norman. 'The guy needs locking up. We can't handle that.'

'I need to call Stella,' said Slater. 'They're raiding Keeling's office and home today. I'll see if she can get them to arrest him on suspicion.'

'There are services up ahead,' said Norman. 'Pull in here. I'll get us coffee while you make your call.'

Fifteen minutes later, Norman climbed back into the car with two coffees.

'What did Stella say?' he asked.

'Apparently, Keeling has so much pornography on his home laptop he's already been taken in for questioning. They've also found three mobile phones with messages suggesting he uses the name "Josh", or simply "J" with all his girlfriends, and photos sent to him from those girlfriends confirm he likes them young.'

'Jeez, he sounds like a real charmer,' said Norman.

'That's a more polite description than the one Stella used.'

'It's got to be quite a result for her,' said Norman. 'It certainly won't do her chances of keeping her job any harm.'

'I can't believe this all started over a text message,' said Slater.

'Yeah, but it isn't quite finished yet,' said Norman. 'We still need to get us a Tim.'

NEITHER OF THEM had said a word for about ten minutes.

'I think I owe you an apology,' said Norman, quietly.

'What?'

'I owe you an apology.'

'Why?'

'You've been asking after me because you're worried about me, and I've behaved like a spoilt brat and snapped your head off every time.'

'Don't worry about it,' said Slater. 'We all have off days now and then.'

'Yeah, but I've had them just about every day.'

Slater nodded, thoughtfully.

'Now you mention it, I suppose there have been a few more than normal,' he conceded.

'Don't pretend, Dave, I've been all over the shop, and I've been taking it out on you.'

'It's okay, I'm not going to hold it against you.'

'But you deserve an explanation.'

'Look, if you don't want to share whatever it is, that's okay,' said Slater.

'But I do,' said Norman. 'Jeez, you're the only real friend I have. I owe it to you, to be honest.'

'You felt I was being nosey. I understand. You don't ow—.'

'For God's sake! Will you just pipe down, and listen?' snapped Norman. Then, contritely, 'Shit! There, you made me do it again.'

'I'm sorry. I promise I won't say another word.'

'Thank you,' said Norman. 'The thing is, I have something I want to share. No, make that something I need to share with you.'

Slater waited a few seconds, but Norman didn't say anything else, so he took his eyes off the road long enough to glance across at his partner. He was just in time to catch Norman wiping a tear from his cheek.

'Jesus, Norm, what is it?' he asked.

Norman shook his head. 'Give me a minute.'

Slater tried to focus on his driving, but he couldn't stop himself from keeping half an eye on Norman.

After a while, Norman let out a long, sad-sounding sigh.

'I'm sorry,' he said, finally. 'This is difficult.'

'No worries,' said Slater. 'Just take your time, I'm not going anywhere.'

'I'm not with Jane anymore.'

Slater was so surprised by this shocking news he didn't quite know what he should say.

'Every couple has a barney now and then,' he said, helplessly. 'It'll blow over.'

'No, that's not it,' said Norman. 'We haven't had an argument, and you forget we're not a couple. We're a guy and a woman with three kids. That's a quintet. It's not the same thing at all.'

Once again Slater didn't know how to respond, but this time he kept his empty words to himself.

'Jane always puts the kids first,' said Norman. 'I knew it was going to be like that, and of course, it's how it should be. The thing is they miss their dad.'

'She's not going back to him?' asked Slater, unable to keep the shock from his voice. 'You were nearly murdered because of him!'

'That was then, and this is now,' argued Norman. 'He paid for what he did. Now three kids need their father. I think it's for the best.'

'Bloody hell, Norm. Are you sure this is the right thing to do?'

'I have no rights when it comes to Jane or those kids, and I certainly don't have the right to stop a family being a family, do I?'

'Yeah, but... I thought you and Jane were made for each other.'

Norman smiled a sad little smile.

'I thought so, too. I reckon there's probably a parallel universe where that's true, but I'm afraid that's not the one I live in.'

Slater reached across and patted Norman's leg. 'Mate, I am so sorry,' he said.

Norman heaved a big, shuddering, sigh.

'Yeah, me too,' he said with a catch in his voice. 'We had some good times, though, and at least we didn't part on bad terms.'

'I've been rambling on about Stella and me, and how great things are,' said Slater, guiltily, 'and all the time you've been hurting... I'm sorry.'

'Don't be an idiot, you had no idea. Anyway, I'm the one who's been asking about you and Stella.'

They drove on in silence for a while, until Norman spoke again.

'When I was a kid, my mum used to sing this song to me. I can't recall the verse, but I never forgot the chorus. It went "Que sera, sera".'

'Whatever will be, will be,' added Slater.

'That's the one,' said Norman, wistfully. 'Whatever will be, will be, the future's not ours to see. I certainly didn't see this future coming, that's for sure.'

'D'you want a minute, or d'you want to talk?' asked Slater. 'We can stop for another coffee if you want.'

'To be honest, I'm all coffeed out,' said Norman. 'Can we just keep driving for a bit?'

'Sure we can. You just say the word if you want to stop.'

37

As they pulled off the road into the lay-by, they looked towards the old car where Tim lived.

'Jesus!' said Slater, slamming on the brakes.

'Wow! That must have been some fire,' muttered Norman.

Where the battered old car had stood just yesterday morning, there was now a blackened, charred, hulk. Wisps of smoke spiralled upwards, and a strong stench of burnt rubber served to emphasise what must have happened. There was a movement from beyond the car, and Kelly Sellars stumbled into view.

'Come on, Norm,' said Slater, throwing open his car door. 'We'd better see what's going on.'

They walked quickly across to Sellars who seemed to be in a daze.

'What the hell's happened here?' asked Slater.

'What does it look like?'

'Was it vandals?' asked Norman.

'I have no idea,' said Sellars.

'Where's Tim? Is he okay? He wasn't in the car when it—'

'There's no sign of him anywhere around here, but as to where he is, I don't know.'

Slater was circling around the car, trying to figure what might have happened.

'This is all a bit vague, Kelly,' said Norman. 'You don't really expect us to believe you have no idea where your brother is, do you?'

'Honestly, I knew nothing about this until I heard a fire engine siren and saw the smoke. I ran over here, but the car was a raging inferno by then.'

'What about Tim?'

'I dunno. At first, I thought he might have been caught in the car, but the fire crew assured me no-one had been trapped inside. They hadn't seen anyone around when they arrived. They did say they thought the fire had been started on purpose, but that's all they told me.'

Slater had rejoined them after his circuit around the burnt-out wreckage.

'Tim did this, didn't he?' he demanded.

'I couldn't say.'

'Couldn't say, or won't say?' asked Norman.

'When he spoke to us earlier he said something about getting away with it, and moving on,' said Slater.

'You know more than me, then,' said Sellars. 'I told you before, I might be his brother, but he doesn't confide in me.'

'Yeah, well you can tell that to the police,' said Norman.

'Police?'

'Conspiracy to murder,' said Norman. 'I told you before.'

'But he hasn't murdered anyone!'

Norman's face was inches from Sellars.

'He coaxed a young lad to stab his own father,' he snarled. 'You knew all about that, and you've helped him do it. Fortunately for you and your brother we got to the kid before he could stab anyone, but even so you're in some seriously deep shit.'

'And, for your information,' added Slater. 'Your brother was wrong about Jason Crothers. He wasn't the man he claimed he saw at the crash that night.'

'No. You're wrong. Tim knows what he saw.'

'Oh Tim saw a man at the scene, and he saw him move the body, but he couldn't be sure who he saw. He assumed he knew who it was because that's who he wanted it to be.'

'But he saw the contact on the phone. It was "J" for Jason.'

'But it wasn't "J" for bloody Jason. Jason Crothers was miles away from here. He had nothing to do with that crash!' roared Slater.

'Yes, but he still caused the death of Tim's wife and daughter.'

'Oh yes, about that,' said Norman. 'It seems Tim forgot to mention that the police carried out a thorough investigation and couldn't find a shred of evidence to back up the allegation.'

'What? I didn't know that.'

'So says you.'

'He didn't tell me that. I told you before he tells me hardly anything. Anyway, even if he didn't touch her, Jason still caused their deaths.'

'Jeez, listen to yourself,' said Norman. 'You're as bad as your sick-in-the-head brother.'

'He has good reason to be sick in the head!' snapped Sellars.

'Oh, so that makes it okay, then does it?' asked Norman. 'Anyone who's had a tragedy in their life can find a victim to bump off, and that will make it all better, will it?'

'An eye for an eye,' argued Sellars.

'So, by your reckoning, it will be just fine if Mia Crothers comes for you now, right?' asked Slater.

'Well, I—'

'Don't you see?' said Slater. 'Doing it your way, it never ends, does it? What sort of world is that?'

'I can't waste any more breath on this guy,' said Norman. 'We have to find Tim.'

'You won't find him,' Sellars assured them.

'We have to.'

'Tim told you he'd get away with it, and he has.'

'Where's he gone, Kelly?' said Slater. 'Where can we find him?'

'You don't get it, do you?' said Sellars. 'I have no idea where he is. He hasn't told me.'

'But he's your brother for God's sake!'

'You think that makes a difference? As far as he is concerned, I'm a liability. I always have been, even when we were kids.'

'Are you telling me he's left you to face the consequences on your own?'

'It's not the first time.'

'You must have some idea where he is,' said Norman. 'Come on, think. What's he going to do next?'

'He'll probably do what he's good at.'

'What's that?'

'Hiding.'

'Is that supposed to be funny?'

'I'm sorry, but you've lost this one,' said Sellars. 'My brother doesn't call himself The Invisible Man for nothing.'

'The police will be looking for him,' said Slater, 'and they'll start by questioning you.'

'I can't tell them any more than I can tell you.'

'Yeah? Well, we'll see about that, won't we?'

'Come on, Dave,' said Norman. 'He's not going to help us, and we have somewhere else we need to be.'

38

'You think he sent the text by accident? Are you serious?' asked, Lizzie Becker.

'We have no reason to believe this man intended to upset you,' explained Norman. 'Jason Crothers was the person he wanted to hurt, not you.'

'He was quite open about his desire to get even with Jason,' added Slater. 'But there's nothing to suggest he ever intend any harm to you.'

'And you say he saw the accident?' asked Lizzie.

'He saw the aftermath of the accident.'

'But he can prove Lilly wasn't driving?'

'That's what he told us,' said Norman.

'So I can finally clear her name?'

'As long as the police can find enough evidence to build a case.'

'But, if this man saw what happened?'

'The thing is he's disappeared,' explained Slater. 'We have no idea where he is, or where he's heading.'

'The police are searching for him,' added Norman.

'But you know what he saw,' she said. 'Can't you tell the police what he told you?'

Norman pulled a face.

'Yeah, we can, and we will, but it's hearsay evidence. It's not as good as the real thing, and it's possible it might not even be admissible.'

Lizzie looked a beaten woman.

'I was really hoping,' she said, sadly.

Norman smiled a sad little smile.

'I know,' he said, kindly. 'We're disappointed, too. If only we'd realised the guy was going to disappear.'

'You couldn't have known that,' she said.

Slater looked away, guiltily. Sure, they couldn't have known for certain, but they should have guessed what might happen once Sellars had told them his plan.

'So this man Keeling,' said Lizzie. 'You say he and Lilly were... he was grooming her, is that right?'

Norman squirmed in his seat.

'Well, it must have started like that,' he said, uncomfortably, 'but it seems they had moved on past that stage.'

She looked at him, startled.

'Oh my God. You mean, she was—'

'I'm sorry, Lizzie, but it appears Lilly was a willing partner,' said Norman. 'That doesn't excuse what he did, and because Lilly was below the age of consent, he'll have no defence when it comes to court.'

'Did Jason Crothers know?'

'We don't know for sure,' said Norman. 'That's something the police are going to have to find out.'

'But you think...'

'We believe he must have known,' said Slater. He would have liked to have told her more, but there was a police investigation ongoing, and he knew they'd probably said more than the police would like as it was.

'How could he have turned a blind eye? He was a family friend,' she said.

. . .

'I DON'T KNOW about you, but I need a drink,' said Slater when they finally left, a few minutes later.

'That's the best idea you've had all day,' said Norman, 'but what about Stella?'

'She's gonna be busy at work tonight,' said Slater. 'So, let's go home and have a few beers.'

EPILOGUE

ne Week Later.

'WHAT D'YOU mean he's going to get away with it?' asked Slater. 'He moved her body, and left her to die. She was only fourteen years old!'

'But we have no evidence, and no witness,' said Stella. 'We all feel as bad about this as you and Norm, but there's nothing we can do if we can't find your witness.'

'What about Jason Crothers? Surely he'll want to save his own neck, won't he?'

'He was more than willing to point the finger at Keeling, but he says he gave Keeling the spare keys to his car.'

'Well, there you are then,' said Slater.

'I'm afraid not. The keys that were found in the car's ignition were not the spare keys. The spare keys are the ones he has at home. Keeling admits he had the keys but didn't use the car that weekend. He says he gave the keys back to Crothers a couple of days later.'

'That's bullshit!'

'Maybe, it is,' agreed Stella, 'but the evidence backs up Keeling's story.'

Slater stared moodily up at the ceiling. He didn't know what to say.

'It's not all bad news,' continued Stella. 'We have enough evidence to charge Keeling, Crothers and Kenny Pearce over the burglary scam, and Keeling is going to be charged with grooming Rosabella Rizzi's daughter.'

'But we told Lizzie Becker the police would find Harvey Sellars,' said Slater.

'Well, we didn't,' said Stella. 'His brother was right when he said he was capable of becoming invisible.'

Slater turned to look at her.

'You're still looking, though, right? I mean he was grooming Mickey Crothers to kill his own father!'

'But no-one actually got hurt, thanks to you and Norm.'

'What does that mean?'

'It means the hunt has been scaled down.'

'You're giving up, and letting him get away with it?'

'We're not giving up, we're scaling down. It's all about money. You know how it works.'

'It's not right,' he said.

'Of course, it's not, but that's how it is.'

Slater slumped back and stared moodily up at the ceiling again.

'I don't know how you put up with it,' he said.

She sighed.

'Yes, but you forget, it's only for another week.'

'I'm sorry,' he said, reaching for her hand. 'I know you'd rather be staying on.'

She said nothing for a minute or two.

'I have a suggestion,' she said.

'Okay, let's hear it.'

She reached across and turned off the bedside lamp, plunging the bedroom into darkness. Then she pulled the quilt up around her shoulders and snuggled up close to him.

'I suggest we stop talking shop and get some sleep.'

'Okay, but I can't promise to drop off straight away,' he said, slipping an arm around her.

BOOKS BY P.F. FORD

SLATER AND NORMAN MYSTERIES

Death Of A Temptress

Just A Coincidence

Florence

The Wrong Man

The Red Telephone Box

The Secret Of Wild Boar Woods

A Skeleton In The Closet

The Kidney Donor

What's In A Name?

A Puzzle Of Old Bones

A Fatal Deception

Wrongly Convicted

Deceptive Appearances

The Invisible Man

ABOUT THE AUTHOR

A late starter to writing after a life of failures, P.F. (Peter) Ford spent most of his life being told he should forget his dreams, and that he would never make anything of himself without a "proper" job.

But then a few years ago, having been unhappy for over 50 years of his life, Peter decided he had no intention of carrying on that way. Fast forward a few years and you find a man transformed by a partner (now wife) who believed dreamers should be encouraged and not denied.

Now, happily settled in Wales, Peter is blissfully happy sharing his life with wife Mary and their four rescue dogs, and living his dream writing fiction (and still without a "proper" job).

www.pfford.co.uk

Printed in Great Britain
by Amazon